THE SHAPE OF HOME
An Anthology of Middle Eastern and North African Voices

Edited by
Amber Bliss & K. Parr

Cover Design by
Rashaa Al-Sasah

WEST
WARWICK
PUBLIC
LIBRARY

2022

THE SHAPE OF HOME
An Anthology of Middle Eastern and North African Voices
Edited by Amber Bliss & K. Parr

West Warwick Public Library
1043 Main Street
West Warwick, RI 02893
www.wwpl.org

This project was made possible by an American Rescue
Plan Humanities Grant. American Rescue Plan:
Humanities Grants for Libraries is an initiative of the
American Library Association (ALA) made possible with
funding from the National Endowment for the Humanities
(NEH) through the American Rescue Plan Act of 2021.

NATIONAL
ENDOWMENT
FOR THE
HUMANITIES

Acknowledgements

We want to thank our friends at the American Library Association for the generous funding that made this project possible. Thank you to our new partner, Community Libraries of Providence, for joining us on this endeavor. Your support has been invaluable, and we look forward to a lasting and productive partnership. Writing is often a solitary pursuit, but good writing takes community, and we were lucky to have incredible guest authors and publishing professionals share their experiences and knowledge with our writers. Endless thanks to Dima Alzayat, Rajia Hassib, Omar El Akkad, Mai Al-Nakib, Leila Aboulela, Sahar Mustafah, and Carlisle Webber. This project may be over, but what you taught our students will last throughout their careers. Thanks also to our wonderful cover artist, administrative powerhouse, and co-director of the press, Rashaa Al-Sasah. A huge shout-out goes to our new copyeditor Kristen Bezner. We don't know how we used to do this without you! Finally, thank you to all the staff at West Warwick Public Library for picking up extra work in order to free up time for this project and for putting in countless hours of proofreading to make it the best it can be.

Contents

Fiction & Poetry

Since Melissa's companionship provided Roodi with a fleeting sense of belonging, she no longer wants immigrant friends like herself. As both women go through major life changes, their relationship is put to the test.

Even after living in the States for more than a decade, Esma still relies on her husband to navigate American society. Will this immigrant mother find a way to become more independent or will she remain set in her ways?

Zeina struggles to maintain her composure at a family barbeque as her world falls apart.

What is the secret to making hummus that tastes of home?

Introduction

The Shape of Home is our fourth grant-funded community writing project, and it is our first time co-editing in partnership with the Community Libraries of Providence. Being able to work together with such a dedicated and supportive group of creators has been an incredible experience, and the things we've learned from our writers and each other have allowed us to expand the Press and the reach of this program. It has been an honor to be able to practice some of the lessons about community and teamwork our authors have been teaching us all summer.

Each group of writers we work with offers us the incredible opportunity to learn and see and feel glimpses of places and experiences different from our own and to grow from it, which is the true gift of literature. That same gift is available to you all in the pages of this anthology through the incredibly personal and passionate stories our creators have shared. The authors have delved into moments of pain, joy, triumph, and failure to bring something genuine to the public, and they did it by supporting, encouraging, teaching, and commiserating with each other.

So, pick up a copy and explore the stories and poetry of these incredible women, and we assure you, what you take away from the pages will be well worth the read.

~AMBER BLISS &
K. PARR
August 2022

Pigeons and Peregrines

by
Maryam Ghatee

Perhaps people cry when they're angry

Because their souls cannot speak

-Malack Jallad

Cringing at the sound of Dia's wails, Roodi flipped through her mental checklist of reasons babies cry. Her mother-in-law held the vestibule door open for her to push the stroller into the apartment lobby. Although Roodi had shown her the push plate that opened the door automatically, Mazyar's mother still insisted on helping in her own little ways.

A delivery guy with a loaded hand truck disappeared into one of the elevators. Before they could press the call button, the second lift's doors slid open to reveal a familiar blonde—Melissa. Roodi felt a pang of sadness at the sight of her friend, whose expression broke into a smile.

"Oh. My. Goodness," Melissa shrieked. "It's Nadia!"

Dia was born during Melissa's winter break, while she was in Westchester County for her engagement party followed by a ski trip to Vermont with her fiancé. Since her return, Roodi had only met with her once: at their favorite café on Thames Street while her mother-in-law watched Dia.

Roodi folded back the stroller canopy and stepped aside to show off her daughter. "We've been calling her Dia." She didn't explain it was because her mother-in-law thought Nadia sounded too Arabic.

Roodi caught a waft of Melissa's perfume as she bent over Dia, who stopped crying at the sight of the strange face. Roodi hugged herself and took another step back. She was still sweaty from pushing the stroller and hadn't showered in two days. A glance at Melissa, who could list *chic* as a natural trait, made Roodi wish she was wearing something better than a sweatshirt and yoga pants. She ran fingers through her matted hair, which sent a familiar tingle through her C-section scar.

Melissa *oohed* and *aahed* and made faces at Dia before straightening.

Roodi sensed a hug coming her way, and quickly said, "This is Mazyar's mother." She regretted the introduction immediately. "She doesn't speak any English."

Melissa shook hands with Mazyar's mother. "Melissa," she said a little too loudly, as if taking it up a few decibels would bridge the language gap.

Roodi studied her friend's flawless face but failed to find any hints of condescension.

Melissa's eyes twinkled as she grasped to recall something. "Man Melissa hastam," she said in her thick American accent.

Her mother-in-law searched Roodi's eyes in confusion.

"She speaks a little Farsi," Roodi told her, and then repeated what Melissa had said.

Her mother-in-law's expression expanded into a toothy smile.

Melissa turned to Roodi. "You look *great*. How *are* you?"

"Sleep deprived," Roodi replied brightly, trying to match Melissa's tone. "But Mazyar's mother has been a great help. I don't know how I will manage when she leaves."

This wasn't entirely true. Sure, her mother-in-law had done most of the cooking, but it also meant Roodi had spent more bleary-eyed time in grocery stores searching for a specific ingredient so they could have meals that were far more elaborate than anything she and Mazyar normally cooked. Mazyar also felt the pressure to entertain his mother since it was her first time in America, so his weekends were spent driving her to Washington, D.C. and other local attractions while Roodi stayed home with the baby. Her mother-in-law's visa allowed her to stay for another three months, but she wanted to be in her own house before the vernal equinox to prepare for the Persian New Year.

Roodi was looking forward to her departure. At least Mazyar would be home more often.

"Well, if there's anything—*anything*—I can do, let me know," Melissa said.

Roodi wanted to tell her friend how much she had missed her. "I know you're overwhelmed with your qualifying exam." She swallowed hard. "And the wedding planning." She winced at the discomfort from her scar.

"But I'd love to help," Melissa insisted.

"Well, Dia doesn't have a routine yet, so you'd have to come over."

The elevator dinged. Roodi pulled the stroller back to let the delivery guy roll his empty hand truck away.

"Of course," Melissa said. "I'll text you when I can stop by."

"Are you free any night this week? We can meet before Mazyar's mom leaves."

"How about tomorrow night? There's a new sushi place downtown."

Roodi nodded enthusiastically. It would be nice to be a normal adult rather than an exhausted mother for a change.

Melissa glanced at her phone. "I have to run." Roodi tensed when Melissa hugged her, but her best friend didn't seem to notice as she turned to Mazyar's mother. "Nice to meet you," she said word by word. "Hoda-hafes."

Mazyar's mother put her right hand to her chest and leaned forward in the Iranian way of respect. "Bye-bye," she said childishly.

Roodi watched Melissa until she vanished behind the door to the parking garage. The elevator doors slid open again and her sixth-floor, middle-aged neighbor whose name she couldn't recall stepped into the lobby with two overly excited skinny dogs—Italian greyhounds, he had once told Roodi in the courtyard.

Mazyar's mother let out a shriek and leapt to the other side of the stroller to distance herself from the ritually unclean beasts. The dogs jumped and yapped at the sudden movement, and Dia started wailing again. The neighbor grimaced as he pulled the dogs away.

Roodi waved a tired arm between the closing elevator doors in time to halt them so they could get inside. Mazyar's mother was never going to get used to the sight of dogs, but Roodi was now used to her reaction. She stuck a pacifier into Dia's mouth and jabbed the button for their floor.

"Your friend seems nice," Mazyar's mother said in Farsi.

"She is. We met in the elevator when we moved here three years ago," Roodi explained. "When she found out we are Iranian, she asked me to teach her Farsi. Her then-boyfriend, now-fiancé, is Iranian—second generation. His name is Sohrob, but she calls him Rob."

Mazyar's mother seemed satisfied with Sohrob's heritage. "Will you continue to tutor her?"

They arrived at their floor and exited the elevator. Roodi shook her head. "I hadn't realized how difficult it is to teach Farsi. Melissa only picked up a few greetings."

Roodi's explanation was valid, but she knew Mazyar would have told an entirely different story. From the beginning he believed Melissa would give up on Farsi lessons if she got engaged, while Roodi insisted that her friend would keep it up for her future children. A week after Sohrob proposed, Melissa canceled the lessons.

Roodi would have given anything to erase Mazyar's smirk.

Mazyar's mom unlocked the apartment door. "She's more cultured than the one who visited last week— Lebanon?"

"Lubna," Roodi said. "She's from Morocco."

"Yes. I like this one better. Be wary of a person who observes the hijab when it's not mandatory." Years of theocracy had blurred the lines of religion and politics for Iranians.

"Lubna is OK, she just doesn't fit in. She never joins the team after work." Roodi suspected that Lubna had a problem with establishments that serve alcohol. She didn't drink alcohol either, but always showed up. *That's how people advance their careers*, Melissa had taught her.

***

Roodi salivated from re-reading the menu. Nursing Dia left her constantly hungry. She couldn't have raw fish, so she narrowed her options down to teriyaki salmon or vegetarian maki and set the menu aside. Through the storefront window she could see Melissa outside, still on her phone.

Melissa had taught Roodi everything she knew about sushi. In fact, everything she knew about food other than Iranian cuisine, pasta, and hamburgers came from Melissa. When Melissa tried to pay her for their first lesson, Roodi had habitually declined—as was expected in taarof etiquette. "Your willingness to learn my mother tongue is above any payment," she had said.

That was when Melissa suggested lessons over dinner—and she would pay the check. Every Thursday became an amazing adventure into a world she had never experienced from within the Iranian diaspora. Melissa was delighted by Roodi's excitement, and included other jaunts such as rock concerts, musicals, and ball games. Roodi still couldn't get over how the acrobats of Cirque du Soleil defied gravity.

Roodi had checked on Dia and her mother-in-law twice by the time Melissa slipped into the seat across from her.

"I'm sorry. I was nailing down the cake tasting date with my mother."

"No problem. How is Sohrob?" Roodi insisted on using his full name.

"He's doing well. The wedding is set for July 9th! It's at my parents' country club in Westchester County. You'll receive an invite in the mail."

A waitress came to take their orders. Roodi quickly decided on the teriyaki salmon and watched as Melissa charmed the waitress with her bubbling personality as she asked about the menu, and then told her about the sushi station she was planning for her wedding reception.

Roodi's stomach grumbled. She glanced at her phone. No call from her mother-in-law.

Once the waitress jotted down their orders, Melissa continued, "I feel like everything is floating in the air. Five months to the wedding and I'm still not sure about my bridal shower!"

"Let me host it," Roodi blurted. Lubna had thrown her a lackluster baby shower back in October, and while bridal showers were a little different, Roodi knew she could plan a better one than Lubna. Melissa was her best friend, after all.

"Oh, that's so kind of you! Rob's sister was also thinking of doing something, so I will let you know how it works out."

"We could work together." The pre-baby gears started turning in her head. She would book the lounge at their building and plan the food. Rob's sister could do the decor.

The waitress set their food in front of them and Roodi dug in.

Melissa picked up her chopsticks. "When will you go back to work?"

"I don't know yet. Maternity leave is only twelve weeks, and I don't feel comfortable leaving Dia in daycare all day."

"Look into an au pair. My brother and I loved ours growing up."

Roodi was surprised to learn Melissa's mother had hired help when she'd been a homemaker all her life.

"Or a nanny," Melissa added.

"I'm not sure. How can I trust a total stranger when Dia can't even speak yet?" American news was full of horror stories about abusive childcare providers.

"That's why you check their background and references."

Roodi couldn't understand how one could believe the words of a reference they didn't personally know. Americans were quite trusting.

The conversation shifted back to the wedding. Melissa showed her a picture of her first dress fitting. Even with a wedding planner, there were a lot of decisions that Melissa had to make. Weddings in Iran were also quite involved, but since Roodi and Mazyar didn't have any close relatives in America, their marriage had been a small affair officiated at city hall.

The waitress came with the bill and two taiyaki ice creams. "Compliments of the chef," she said to Melissa, "to honor the bride-to-be."

Melissa beamed, and they both thanked the waitress. As Melissa reached for her wallet, the screen of her phone lit up.

"It's my mother again. I have to take it," Melissa said apologetically. She left her card in the bill presenter and went outside.

Roodi wanted to be considerate, but this was supposed to be her night out. She eyed the food Melissa had left to go to waste and sighed as she slid her own card into the leather folder. She finished her dessert, then pulled out her phone to text her mother-in-law, but instead texted Mazyar: I miss you.

***

Roodi Skyped with her parents two hours before the vernal equinox. Internet connections and phone lines slowed down right after the Persian New Year as the diaspora reached out to their loved ones back home. Since coming to the States, she had always been frail around Nowruz, but somehow this year felt even worse. Mazyar had forgotten to take the day off, and Roodi had been too absent-minded to remind him.

When she learned he was too late to put in the vacation request, she had screamed, "You fathered-by-a-dog! How could you miss your child's first Nowruz?" She felt guilty

10

after. Mazyar had always relied on her infallible sense of planning.

On Skype with her parents, she flipped the camera to show them Dia napping in the crib that once belonged to Lubna's son. Her father was a man of few words, so after wishing her a happy New Year, he left the screen, leaving her alone with her mother's grainy image.

"You need to get your hair and eyebrows done, Roodi," her mother said. "It's Nowruz for God's sake."

Roodi scanned her own face in the lower right corner of the screen and let out a sigh. Her mother had been sanding her soul since the American embassy denied her a visa to come visit them.

"I have no time for myself, Maman."

"Hire a babysitter."

"I'll see what I can do." If her mother found out their budget was tight, she would try to send money, which with all the sanctions was exceedingly onerous—more difficult than The Seven Labors of Rostam. Besides, she still didn't like the idea of leaving her child with a stranger.

"You have to find someone before you go back to work."

"I've extended my leave for now." They just needed to get through the next few months until Mazyar graduated from his fellowship and found a job.

"Paid leave?"

Roodi's stomach tightened. She knew where this was headed. "No, Maman. When regular maternity leave is unpaid here, who would pay me for extended leave?"

Her mother pursed her lips. "You'll lose your job."

Roodi clenched her jaw at hearing what she both wished for and feared. It was easy for her mother to criticize—a part-time nanny and two sets of grandparents allowed her to go back to work shortly after Roodi was born. She felt their distance more than ever.

"Happy New Year, Maman."

Roodi disconnected Skype and curled into a ball on the sofa. Tears soaked the paisley cushion.

She woke to the vibration of her phone and felt for it under the cushion. She rolled her eyes at the sight of Lubna's name.

`I know it's your new year. Can I visit you after work? Rachid can pick up Adil from daycare.`

Roodi had been uncomfortable when Lubna planned her baby shower. She read online that showers were customary in America and that a close friend or a family member hosts them. Now that she thought about it, Melissa would have been the appropriate person for hers. But Lubna had quickly set the date and invited Roodi's small guest list—mostly work friends—before Melissa even had a chance to think about it. She still remembered how Melissa had eyed the paper plates Lubna used for the party.

She trembled at the sound of Dia's cries from the bedroom and realized she'd been staring at the blank screen.

She quickly typed: `Not today, it's been rough,` and left to go through the tedious motions of mothering.

After setting Dia down for tummy time, she researched budget-friendly bridal showers to add to her rolling list of ideas. She still hadn't heard from Sohrob's sister. The wedding invitation sat on the kitchen counter next to her laptop. *Although we love your little ones, this is an adult-only affair*, it said. She wasn't sure what they were supposed to do with Dia. "Wedding parties are for the kids" was the saying back in Iran, where kids were allowed to run wild on sugar and the excitement of staying up late.

Mazyar called on his break to wish them a happy New Year. "There's a Nowruz party at the university at eight. Do you want to go?"

"It's too late for Dia," she said. "You can go if you want."

"How about I stay home with her, and you go?" Mazyar said. "You've barely spoken to anyone since my mother left."

Roodi considered this. She had been so sick of farewells each time they moved for Mazyar's training that she hadn't sought the Iranian community when they relocated to Baltimore, knowing this too was temporary. She didn't want to go alone to a party where she knew no one.

"I'd rather stay home with you."

After she hung up, she stared at the blank screen again, willing it to show her a call or message from Melissa. Melissa knew how important Nowruz was to her. They'd only run into each other once since Mazyar's mom left, and Melissa had seemed busier than ever.

A message did come through, but from a number she didn't recognize.

Hi Rudy! This is Sam, Melissa's friend. Rob's sister and I are planning a bridal shower for April 3rd and we heard you want to help. Let me know.

Roodi had met Samantha once in the high-end European boutique she owned in Georgetown, which served super-skinny, super-tall women. Roodi had gasped at the price tags, then sighed in relief when she couldn't fit into anything. Melissa bought a blouse on sale. "What a steal," she had said.

Roodi hadn't realized Sam was such a close friend of Melissa's.

She dismissed the pop-up reminder to balance their family budget and typed in: I'm excited to help. Do you already have a list of tasks? I'm a pretty decent cook.

The reply was immediate.

Will get back to you.

***

A week later, Roodi received an electronic invitation titled "Please Join Us for a Bridal Shower in Honor of Melissa Annabelle." It was at 4 p.m. on April 3rd in Potomac. A link to a bridal registry was included and the invite was signed by Gordie and Sam. Roodi hadn't been to a bridal shower before, but found it odd to see a man's name on the invite and wondered why Sohrob's sister wasn't involved.

She texted Sam: I received the electronic invitation. Is there anything I can help with?

She rubbed her scar as she followed the bridal registry link. She clicked on the image of a salad plate to find out how many plates came for the listed $70 price and was shocked to see it was the price for a single plate. Melissa had asked for twelve. She swallowed her anxiety and sorted the items from low to high. Mazyar's call interrupted her.

"How are you?" he asked softly.

"I'm okay. I got an invite to Melissa's bridal shower." She sniffled. "Her friend never got back to me, and they didn't include my name as a host."

"And you're upset? Less of a headache for you."

14

"But I wanted to do something for her." Her throat tightened. "She's like a sister to me and I haven't had time with her since Dia was born."

"Get her a better gift—like a whole set of silverware."

Roodi surveyed the screen of her laptop. "The items on her registry are really expensive, Mazyar. A five-piece set of silverware is more than the whole set we bought at HomeGoods."

Mazyar let out a hearty laugh. "Are they made of gold? If only I could be a fly on the wall when Melissa hosts her first dinner party as a married woman." Melissa was a terrible cook, and the one time she had invited Sohrob's parents for dinner she had asked Roodi and Mazyar to help her with the cooking.

Mazyar continued in a high-pitched voice. "Here is a slice of ready-made mushroom lasagna, but these utensils will make it taste like gratin de crozets et champignons."

Roodi laughed, impressed that he'd remembered the full name of the dish. How she longed for him to be home with her right now. "What do you think I should do? I read online that the norm is to spend $100 per person."

"What are the options?"

Roodi scrolled through the list again. "I can get her four salad plates for $280 plus tax and shipping."

"Do they expect another present for the wedding?" Mazyar asked.

"I don't think so. The article said the bridal shower present is the wedding present. It's not like Iran where you have to give a gift for each ceremony."

"Buy her six, then," Mazyar replied. "Money is grime on the palm. It comes and goes."

*****

Mazyar drove Roodi to Potomac for the bridal shower.

"I'll take Dia to Great Falls Park while you're at the party, so you don't feel like she's too far," he said, but Roodi knew it was because she was scared of the aggressive drivers on I-495.

The first twenty minutes of the trip, Dia wouldn't take the pacifier and Roodi clenched her fists as she cried from her car seat. When Dia finally fell asleep, Roodi racked her brain but failed to come up with anything to talk about with Mazyar. She missed everything about talking like they did before Dia was born—even his natural pessimism. His face looked as tired as she felt. She laced her fingers through his, trying to find reassurance in their silence.

Once they took the exit off the highway, they drove past a golf course and turned into what appeared to be a subdivision. All Roodi saw was woodland behind gates and fences. She caught a glimpse of a building as Mazyar slowed down to check the house number.

"These are mansions," Roodi whispered.

"Yeah," Mazyar said absentmindedly as he eyed the next gate.

Roodi glanced down at the busy paisley print of her loose blouse, dark capris, and flats and wondered if she was stylish enough. She flipped down the sunshade to inspect her face in the mirror and regretted not wearing makeup. Her eyes were tired and her curls were unruly. She wished she could take Mazyar and Dia with her as a way to excuse her appearance.

Mazyar pressed the button of a security access pad at a pair of tall wrought iron gates. No voice came over the intercom, but the gates slowly swung open. Dogwood trees in full bloom lined the stone-paved driveway and the trees beyond donned the bright green of spring. After a bend, an imposing limestone structure appeared with a set of white columns holding up a pediment.

"Welcome to the White House." Mazyar grinned as he surveyed the high-end cars parked along the driveway. "Are Hondas allowed on these premises?"

"How do I look?" she asked nervously.

Still scanning the cars, Mazyar lifted her hand and kissed her knuckles. "You're beautiful, Roodi." He pointed her hand to a sports car as green as a grasshopper. "That one's a Lamborghini."

Roodi rolled her eyes. "Focus, Mazyar. I mean, am I chic enough?"

"This isn't like you, Roodi. You're not here for a fashion show."

The driveway looped around a circular bed of boxwood hedge surrounding a white marble fountain. Mazyar stopped the car at the front steps.

"Will you be okay with Dia?" she asked.

"I'll be fine." He looked past her.

Roodi turned to see Sam coming out of the front double doors wearing golden stiletto sandals and a dark, mint green sleeveless dress. Roodi had left a message at her boutique the week before but hadn't heard back.

Roodi squeezed Mazyar's hand, took a deep breath, and stepped out, carefully holding a wrapped gift box containing six salad plates. As she climbed up the steps, Sohrob's mother, in an off-white knee-length gown, emerged from the building. Both women's left wrists were adorned with corsages of ivory white roses and mint green ribbons.

Sam extended her hand. "I'm glad you made it." Her layered dark hair stylishly framed her made-up face. Her perfect smile bore the emptiness of a retail associate.

Roodi wasn't sure if Sam knew she was the "Rudy" from the text message. She balanced the box to shake hands. "I'm Roodi," she said awkwardly. "We've met before."

"Of course," Sam said, as if she remembered everyone who walked into her boutique. Or everyone she failed to get back to.

Roodi shook hands with Sohrob's mother. "It's nice to see you again."

"Welcome to our house." She offered a tight smile, then turned her attention to another guest climbing the steps.

The foyer led to a highly ornate main hall. An impressive crystal chandelier hung from the center of the room's two-story ceiling over a round dome-patterned Tabriz carpet. A monumental marble stair led to the second floor. Past double doors to the right, she saw a grand room as ornate as the main hall, and the double doors to the left led to a formal dining room. Both rooms were furnished in the style of Louis XVI. In a third room at the far end, a trio of viola, violin, and cello played a familiar piece of Western classical music that Roodi couldn't quite place. The floors of all three rooms were covered by enormous hand-woven Persian rugs in colors that perfectly matched the furniture. Floral arrangements of ivory white roses and soft pink buttercups stood in every corner.

The hum of chatter made the place sound like a women's bathhouse. Servers walked through the halls offering bite-sized hors d'oeuvres to women of different ages. Unable to locate Melissa, and unsure about where to leave the present, Roodi lingered in the main hall with her crossbody bag hanging to her side. She focused on the silk woven into the intricate designs of the Tabriz rug until a woman with dyed blonde hair and a striking resemblance to Sohrob's mother approached her.

She pointed to a side table. "You can leave the present on that table."

Roodi found comfort in her thick Iranian accent.

Her box looked insignificant among the pile of presents. Relieved of the burden, she returned to the woman who extended a bony hand.

"My name is Shahrazad. I am Sohrob's aunt," she continued in English.

With her tan skin and dark curls, people often assumed Roodi was Latina. She shook Shahrazad's extended hand. "I'm Roodabeh," she said in Farsi. Shahrazad's eyebrows rose with slight surprise, so Roodi continued, "I'm a friend of Melissa's."

A professional photographer snapped a picture of them.

Shahrazad beamed. "Roodabeh, wife of Zaal, mother of the legendary Rostam, grandmother of Sohrob," she said, emphasizing each name with satisfaction. "A pure Persian name. My siblings and I also named our children after Shahnameh characters. Mine are Tahamtan and Tahmineh." She pointed to another woman in the crowd. "That's my sister-in-law, who has Arash and Siavash." She surveyed the room but didn't appear to find the other person she was looking for. "My sister named hers Sohrob and Gordafarid."

Sohrob and Gordafarid. The royal warriors from opposing armies who never got beyond flirting. Roodi grinned at the realization that Sohrob's sister was the "Gordie" on the invite. In Iran, every school kid knew the battle of Sohrob and Gordafarid, but no one named their daughter Gordafarid since it was difficult to pronounce even in Farsi.

Shahrazad seemed pleasant, so Roodi decided to stick with her. They found seats in the grand room. Shahrazad knew most of the Iranians in the crowd and started telling Roodi how each person was related to their family. She then asked about Roodi, including where she was from and where she lived.

"Ah, Shiraz, the city of flowers and nightingales," Shahrazad said, her delight reminding Roodi of the sweet aroma of orange blossoms. "I have fond memories of Shiraz in springtime. Do you still go back?"

"I haven't been back in three years." She willed her voice not to break. "Since I got my green card, I try to go back every other year. I still have a few friends there, but I mostly go for my parents." Every visit revealed the empty space of more friends the country had lost to emigration. "When was the last time you visited home, Ms. Shahrazad?"

"I haven't been back since the revolution."

Roodi had only met a few Iranians who had never been back for a visit. Everyone had their own reasons for leaving, so she didn't inquire further. With the turn that the revolution took and then the war, even her own parents had briefly considered leaving Iran, but decided against it. One of her earliest memories was overhearing her mother tell her father, "Whatever hellhole Iran becomes is better than being a foreigner for the rest of my life."

Another woman joined them, extending a plump hand covered with jewels to Shahrazad and then to Roodi. "Is Farah coming?"

"She was invited," Shahrazad said, "but couldn't make it. She hasn't been quite herself since Ali Reza."

"Since Leila, I'd say," the woman replied.

"How much pain and loss can a woman's heart take?" Shahrazad said to Roodi. "First her country, then the Shah—God bless his soul. But how can one continue after losing her own flesh and blood?"

Roodi nodded politely, unable to decipher what Shahrazad meant.

Then the penny dropped.

Ali Reza, the second in succession to the overthrown throne of Iran, committed suicide in January in his home in Boston, ten years after his sister, Leila, ended her own life in Paris. They were talking about the former Empress of Iran. Roodi took in the extravagance that surrounded her, realizing the kind of Iranian Sohrob's family was. Was this the wealth that fueled the fires of an inevitable revolution?

She immediately worried about the photographer and tried to remember if she was in any picture other than the one with Shahrazad. If she was tagged by the current regime's secret police as a royalist, she would be in trouble next time she went to visit her parents. She discreetly rubbed her scar, but it really needed a good scratch, so she asked for the restroom.

On the way she ran into Melissa, exuberant in her soft mint green gown.

"You look lovely, Melissa," she said, eyeing the photographer. "And what a party!"

"Thank you! Sam and Gordie did an amazing job."

Someone called Melissa for a picture and Roodi made a dash for the facilities.

In the privacy of the massive restroom, Roodi rubbed the scar with her fingertips and burst into tears when she recognized the music she'd heard upon arrival as Mozart's Divertimento. She remembered it from the last time she had been to the Baltimore Symphony Orchestra with Mazyar, when she was expecting. Mazyar adored Western classical music, so she always budgeted for season tickets. Except this year—she only bought tickets to one concert, knowing they couldn't go once the baby came.

It was crazy how much she missed spending time with Mazyar, without worrying about this or that. She splashed her face with cold water, then texted him to pick her up before she returned to the gathering.

From the main hall someone tapped a glass to draw everyone's attention. Melissa, Sam, and a very Iranian-looking young woman stood next to the table overflowing with presents, waiting for everyone to gather as servers offered flutes of sparkling wine.

From the back of the crowd, Roodi listened to Gordie toast her sister-to-be, then to Sam toast her sister-in-style. She wished to shrink and disappear when Melissa expressed love and gratitude to both of her *sisters* as well as all the guests. Once people spread out, Roodi caught up with Melissa. "I had a lovely time, but I have to head out. I've left poor Mazyar alone with Dia."

Melissa gave her a peck on the cheek. To her right, Gordie flashed a perfect empty-smile and handed her a small wrapped square box. "Thank you for coming."

The box felt heavy. "Thank you for having me."

As Roodi waited outside for Mazyar, she gently peeled one side of the white wrapping paper to uncover a square engagement photo of Melissa and Sohrob glued to a gray box. She unwrapped the other side to reveal the words *Waterford Crystal* in silver lettering.

At the sound of an approaching engine, she hurled the box over the fence into the woodland before turning back to watch Mazyar pull up to the curb.

"How was it?" Mazyar asked when she climbed into the car.

The smell of dirty diapers overwhelmed her. "I don't want to talk about it."

"Did you get a foot-whipping?" Mazyar asked, half grinning.

"No," Roodi grunted. "You wouldn't understand."

Two of Mazyar's uncles had been tortured by the Shah's secret police only to be executed after the revolution. Even though Sohrob's family ties weren't what upset her, she didn't want to share it with Mazyar. "How did it go?" she asked.

He waved at the brown streaks on his light blue polo shirt, and Roodi noticed its dampness. "We had a diaper explosion," he said. "A change of clothes for me would've been nice."

"Welcome to my everyday fun," Roodi mumbled.

Mazyar pounded the steering wheel. "What is wrong with you, Roodi?"

Dia started crying, and Roodi stiffened. The child's wails were like fingernails against a chalkboard.

"I'm going along with what you want," he continued. "You didn't even ask for my opinion when you extended your leave from work."

"I want what is best for us as a family! A baby cannot be in daycare all day."

"Says who?" Mazyar yelled. "How are we different from all the other working parents out there? You're so absorbed in who-knows-what you haven't even noticed I've been moonlighting twice a week."

The whoosh of a passing golf cart reminded her they were out in public. "Drive us home," she said under her breath.

Mazyar huffed and started the engine.

Dia fell asleep as soon as they reached the highway, but they were both silent until the Baltimore skyline came into view.

"When did you start moonlighting?" Roodi asked, her gaze fixed on the horizon.

"When you showed me that spreadsheet of going on without your income for another six months."

She thought of how absent he had seemed lately. "I'm sorry, Mazyar."

"I don't mind. As long as you're content." Mazyar paused. "But you're not."

"It's just that I used to hang out with Melissa all the time, but as soon as I had Dia she disappeared—like I was no longer worth her time. I no longer know her."

"Pigeon with pigeon, peregrine with peregrine; only the same species fly together," he recited. "What kind of a person do you think she is? She's marrying The Snob." Mazyar had never warmed up to Sohrob and called him Rob the Snob behind his back. Roodi agreed there was an aloofness in Sohrob's demeanor but wrote it off as his second-generationness.

"She's been my best friend for the past three years." Roodi flinched at the thought of everything she had shared with Melissa—the strain the distance had put on her relationship with her parents, the embarrassment of misunderstanding comments at work, her doubts about having a child with their delayed fertility.

Mazyar shrugged as he maneuvered the car over the ancient pavers of Fell Street. "That doesn't necessarily mean she considers you to be her best friend." His words cut like a knife. "Can you get the mail?"

Roodi nodded. She could use a few minutes to herself.

In the mailroom, Roodi's phone vibrated with a text.

Lubna: `Are you home? I'm in front of your building. Made you some mini quiches.`

Not her. Roodi rubbed her scar. The woman had no respect for the boundaries she wanted to set. She stuck her head out and saw Lubna past the glazed entrance, standing tall in her pantsuit and matching wraparound headscarf, her oversized sunglasses on the tip of her nose as she squinted at her phone waiting for Roodi's response. She balanced a container with her other hand. Her son, Adil, ran in and out of sight.

A sudden urge overtook Roodi. She ran and pushed open the vestibule door and hugged Lubna tightly. Next thing she knew, they were in the lounge and she was blabbering about the bridal shower, tears streaming down her face.

Lubna caught Adil staring at Roodi, snapped something in Arabic, and gave him her phone. She then looped her arm through Roodi's and guided her to an armchair farther away.

Roodi wiped her eyes with a tissue Lubna pulled out of her purse. "I mean, what kind of a decent human being would say, 'Will get back to you' and then disappear?" She blew her nose.

"They weren't asking for homemade dolmas." Lubna rubbed her thumb and finger together in the universal sign for money. "They meant if you wanted to contribute to the party."

"How was I supposed to know?!" Roodi looked over her shoulder and caught sight of Adil stealing nervous glances at them.

Lubna placed an arm around Roodi. "It's alright, habibti."

Roodi leaned her head against Lubna's shoulder. "How embarrassing." She picked apart the soaked tissue paper.

"You haven't done anything wrong."

"Roodi?" Mazyar stood across the lounge with Dia. "Why aren't you answering your phone? I got worried."

Roodi pointed to her bag.

Lubna stood to greet Mazyar. "Nadia has grown!" She beamed as she took the baby from his arms.

Hearing Dia's full name, Roodi was reminded of why she'd insisted on the name Nadia. One of the meanings of the name was *hope*—she hoped this child would be the key to belonging in this country.

She left them to splash her face with cold water in the restroom off the lounge. She returned to find Mazyar leaning close to Lubna, who was bouncing Dia on her hip. His brows were furrowed into a frown.

"—attention and community. I suffered from it myself. It could easily go undetected, especially for women like us," Lubna said.

Mazyar caught Roodi's gaze, looking at her as if seeing her for the first time. "When is your follow-up appointment with your Ob-Gyn?"

"December." Roodi glanced between him and Lubna. "Why?"

"Maybe we should go see him," Mazyar said. "About that scar."

"But you already checked it." Her stomach tightened. "It's too much of a hassle to go with Dia."

Lubna interjected, "I'll take a few hours off to watch her."

***

Mazyar gently rocked Dia in a baby swing as he shared a laugh with Lubna's husband, Rachid. From a nearby bench, Roodi and Lubna watched them. The sun shone brighter now that the fog of the antidepressant had dissipated. The playground was full of shouts and laughter of little voices. The older children ran to their parents when an ice cream truck pulled up on the side street.

Roodi had stopped the pills that made her drowsy and didn't bother with the other prescription—now with Dia in daycare she could feel a pressure leaving her body. She thought she'd be terrified, but in those first few days of Dia being away, she'd napped, visited the office to see her supervisor, and caught up with colleagues.

Even though caring for a baby was still a lot of work, Dia actually interacted with her surroundings and was no longer a tiny demanding *thing*. She seemed interested in Adil swinging high next to her.

"He's been crazy about swings since he learned how to pump his legs at daycare," Lubna said. She tore a piece of bread into pieces and threw it to the pigeons nearby.

"We were lucky there was a spot for Dia; I would never rely on online reviews. The staff in the infant room are amazing. Chatting with them at drop-off makes my morning."

Lubna nodded. "What we like about the place is that the families come from different backgrounds. We made friends with some parents in Adil's group."

"How do you manage it all, Lubna?" Roodi said. "I'm anxious about returning to work."

"I can't lie—it's not easy. But you won't find your place in this country if you stay home. Work is more than a paycheck."

Lubna had just returned from maternity leave when Roodi first met her at work, and she now felt guilty for judging her. Happy Hours started when daycares closed.

There was a scuffle at the swings and Rachid rushed over to their crying son and said something in Arabic. Adil's shorts were wet.

Lubna handed him the car key. "The glove compartment."

To avoid the weight of Adil's embarrassment, Roodi sauntered over to the swings. Her heart soared when Dia released a tiny squeal from Mazyar's tickles.

Mazyar looked at her brightly. "Why haven't we been hanging out with them?"

Roodi smiled but avoided his eyes as she adjusted the blanket that filled the empty space between Dia's tiny body and the back of the swing. "We'll see more of them," she said. Baltimore was going to be home now that Mazyar had accepted a position in the same hospital.

Emergency averted, Adil went back to swinging and Roodi settled on the bench again.

"Thank you, Lubna."

Lubna looked at her in surprise. "For what?"

"For hosting my baby shower." Her voice quivered. "For reaching out, even when I was terrible at responding."

Lubna laughed pleasantly. "I'm sure you would do the same for a new mother."

Roodi raised her gaze to the clear sky. A bird soared in the distance. Time for a new chapter of her life, a chapter that began when she received a wedding invitation and replied, "Declines with Regret."

Beyond Repair

by
Gizem Zencirci

They say that you cannot fix what is already broken

But who decides what is?

-Malack Jallad

Esma is the kind of woman who can hold a grudge against a vacuum cleaner.

Right now, she is cleaning her house—while listening to Sezen Aksu, of course—on this unusually warm October day.

She does the dishes and wipes down the counters.

She washes some apples and strawberries and lines them on a clean towel. She will later put them in small storage boxes like she learned from Instagram. An easy snack the girls can have when they come home from school. *Saves so much time!* the peppy mom had said.

She boils water for tea.

She folds the clean laundry and organizes her daughters' clothes for their various activities: ballet, soccer, drama.

She considers throwing in another load of laundry.

And finally, she sweeps and mops the floors.

As she leans the broom and the mop in the corner of the kitchen, she hears a car pulling up the driveway. She rushes to the window and sees Artan's metallic blue sedan.

What is her husband doing at home at this hour? He was supposed to go back to work after attending Nari's parent-teacher conference.

Esma rushes back to the bedroom to put on a fresh blouse. She checks herself in the mirror. Her dull skin and tired eyes surprise her. She spritzes some perfume and applies lip gloss, then picks up a pair of small pearl earrings and holds them next to her face.

Her mother's voice pops in her mind: *Don't be too eager!* Esma puts the earrings down in their little ceramic bowl.

But then, wouldn't her mother also say *keep a little mystery?* Esma puts on the earrings as she walks down the stairs.

"What's wrong?" Esma asks when Artan walks through the door.

"Nothing. I have a headache." Artan avoids her gaze.

He drops his keys on the small table next to the door, and dust rises when they hit the surface. Esma makes a mental note of it. Artan takes off his shoes and places them neatly next to each other. The familiarity of this gesture warms Esma's heart.

He goes into the kitchen to drink a glass of water. Esma follows him and leans on the door frame. It's weird to see him in the middle of the day—without the endless babble of the girls and conversations about coordinating their after-school activities.

She can't contain herself any longer. "What did the teacher say? Did something happen at school? Is she having trouble? I have been making sure that they both do their homework."

Artan's expression is blank as he sets the glass of water down. He turns to her with a smile.

"Nari is doing well. She is ahead in math and her grades are excellent. The teacher praised her friendship skills too. She said we are doing a good job raising a social butterfly," Artan explains.

Esma wrinkles her brows. "A social butterfly? What does that mean?"

"It means she is popular and has a lot of friends." His tone is a mix of patience and exasperation.

"Oh, I see," Esma responds.

Artan looks as if there is something else. He finally says, "Let's have some tea," and sits down at the kitchen table.

Esma pours the bitter black tea into tiny tea glasses. She opens a box of cookies and organizes them neatly on a small plate. She always has a stash in her cupboard for sudden guests—not that anyone ever visits unexpectedly.

She brings two cups of tea and sets the plate of cookies between them.

Artan mutters, "Eline sağlık."

Esma longs to break the silence. "It's warm today, almost like spring. We could go for a walk. The girls won't be back for another hour."

Artan nods quietly. He stares at the tree in their backyard. The leaves are beginning to turn a bitter red. The changing colors are one of the few things that ground Esma in this New England town.

Artan turns his attention back to her. He looks around the spotless kitchen. He points to the broom and mop, hugging each other like young lovers, leaning against the kitchen wall.

"Why don't you use the vacuum cleaner?"

"You already know. I don't like it."

Artan shakes his head. "You are impossible! Why are you never content with appliances?"

Esma lowers her cup. "I *am* content. Just not with this one."

Her husband had purchased the vacuum cleaner as a Mother's Day gift about three years ago. He was lucky Esma didn't share her mother's aversion toward receiving household appliances as gifts. Only jewelry, perfumes, or an expensive dinner were worthy of her mother's approval. Esma still cringed when she remembered the hushed, late-night argument her parents had the one time her father made the grave mistake of purchasing her a toaster. It was their wedding anniversary for God's sake!

She wasn't like her mother. Esma had nothing against getting a vacuum cleaner as a gift, but she did have something against this vacuum cleaner.

Not only was it too heavy to maneuver, it also didn't suck the dirt and dust properly. Often Esma ended up using a sweeper instead, just like she did this morning. Esma longed for the European brands she could get back home—sleek, effortless, and pretty gadgets her friends from high school seemed able to afford despite the country's everlasting economic difficulties. None of them could understand why the European brands were not actually considered brands in America.

Esma says, "I think it's time to buy a new one. What do you say?"

Artan purses his lips and grabs a cookie, looks at it, and puts it down.

Esma wishes she hadn't eaten a second cookie. She shifts in her chair and straightens her back. "What did the teachers say? How is Nari doing at school?"

"I already told you. She is fine."

"What is it then? What's wrong with you today?"

Artan takes a deep breath and starts slowly, "Esma, canım, we can't buy new stuff if I take time off work every time the girls have a meeting."

"You could have mentioned it earlier if you couldn't make it."

"We both know that you weren't going to go, don't we?"

Esma doesn't have a response. She knows what would have happened if she'd gone to the meeting. The teacher would have been frustrated by her English, and Esma would have been confused by the teacher's strange turns of phrase. She looks down at the floral pattern of her blouse, rolling the edge of her skirt in between her fingers.

Artan takes a purple brochure out of his pocket and slides it across the table.

Esma can make out the words:

INTERMEDIATE ENGLISH LESSONS—ALL ARE WELCOME!

"It's not that difficult. Just give it a try." His voice is softer now, almost loving.

Her stomach churns. Was she not doing enough for her husband, their daughters, the house, and her mother-in-law who lived two hours away, but visited regularly? So what if she couldn't speak much English? She had so many responsibilities and she fulfilled them all: the shopping, the cooking, the cleaning, the laundry, the yard work. It had taken her quite a long time to accept that she had to do everything herself—without any household help, that is. And she had done everything, for fifteen years, and this is the response she gets from him?

Esma was on the brink of independence when she met Artan in an Aegean town. They were both on vacation: him taking a solo break from the compulsory tour of relatives, and her taking a vacation with her college friends before embarking on post-graduate life. She had a job lined up at an advertising agency. She was looking for apartments to rent in Istanbul. She certainly had no plans to get married and move overseas. But then she had fallen in love, and everything changed. When Esma first told her mother about Artan, her mother had said, *Summer love does not make a marriage*. She would hate to prove her mother right.

***

The purple brochure takes its place among the envelopes, letters, homework sheets, and other paraphernalia on the command center in the kitchen. Despite her meticulous attention to detail, Esma doesn't touch this corner of their otherwise spotless home. It is Artan who periodically goes through each piece of paper, paying bills, filing documents, sending letters, and recycling the rest.

Esma keeps putting the brochure at the bottom of the pile but every morning she finds it at the top. This dance continues until her mother-in-law comes to visit for Thanksgiving. Her mother-in-law is a kind woman hardened by years of scraping by to raise her two sons, Artan and his adrift younger brother. She has moved to a neighboring state—to be closer to her relatives, she had said—but she still visits regularly. Esma doesn't mind; in fact, she enjoys her unassertive companionship.

A couple of days after her arrival, Artan sits down with his mother at the kitchen table. She brings a yellow envelope and a black ajanda worn out from decades of use. The ajanda is bursting with information: passwords, doctors' names, phone numbers—some scribbled, others written with big bold letters. It's as if Esma is the only witness to a sacred ritual between mother and son. His mom arranges the paperwork, explains, and listens; Artan talks on the phone, fills out the forms, and takes care of things. In between tasks, she tells him about her various ailments and updates him about friends and relatives.

When they are almost done, Esma serves three small cups of coffee and joins them at the table. Her mother-in-law is grateful.

She pats her son's hand affectionately and her eyes grow teary. "May Allah be content with you. What would I have done otherwise?"

Artan beams at his mother. "Don't even mention it. There is no need to get emotional."

He is in his element: caring and confident. But Esma's heart flutters for him. She sees him neither as a dutiful son nor as an annoying husband, but as a young boy who had to grow up long before his time.

He turns to Esma and says, "I'll tackle the papers over there next weekend, OK?"

***

Esma parks, grabs her purse, and runs across the church parking lot. She is late, and it is only the first meeting. This is unlike her, but it isn't her fault, really. This morning she drove her mother-in-law to a doctor's appointment—nothing serious, just some routine checkups and blood work—and then she took Suna to her ballet practice, which was, of course, also at a church—but one that was across town.

"This better be worth it," she mumbles to herself as she pushes through the double doors. The church is an old and ornate building. Through the open door Esma can see a pottery class for seniors is being held in the main chamber. She keeps following signs that direct her to one of the side meeting rooms.

Inside the room seven adults sit in a circle; some smiling anxiously, and others playing on their phones. Esma takes one of the remaining seats and sits with her chin up and back straight. As she looks around the circle, she politely makes eye contact with anyone who glances her way. Were they newcomers, or had they been living here for more than a decade like her?

Everyone is dressed up in clean and ironed clothes. The men wear shiny shoes and jackets, and the women—other than a woman with a headscarf and beautiful green eyes—each have a full face of makeup. The regular congregation of the church would never be this elegant, not even on a Sunday.

Thanks to Hollywood, most people back home imagined America as a modern and fanciful place. Each time Esma truthfully answered her cousins' endless questions about cars, fashion, restaurants, schools, and streets over here, she felt like she was crushing their dreams.

But then there were also other relatives—like her own mother—who found nothing valuable about life in America. When Esma explained her decision to marry Artan, her mother had asked, "Why would you move someplace you would be treated like a second-class citizen?"

Her dad had said nothing. He knew that love made people do the oddest things.

Both of her parents were impressed when Artan came bearing gifts and charming everyone as he always did.

During her first few months in America, she had the naive enthusiasm of a tourist. The roads were so wide, and supermarkets offered so many choices! People smiled and said hi to strangers, which she took as a sign of hospitality. The best part was that men didn't stare her down in the streets at all; in fact, she wasn't even sure if they were aware of the presence of her body.

Artan took her to Boston, and even to New York, to see the sights. "Our honeymoon," he called it. They saw a Broadway show together. Esma was mesmerized with the music, dance, and performance despite the embarrassment caused by the almost-naked bodies.

Eventually Artan had to go back to his job. He would kiss her on the forehead every morning and Esma would find things to do. On the weekends, Artan would take her out to try new restaurants and would sometimes invite his college friends over. Her mother-in-law would host groups of women—some about Esma's age, some a little older—for tea parties. The women were friendly, almost too friendly, at times pulling her into different cliques and factions. Esma learned the ins and outs of immigrant life in the suburbs from them—where to do the grocery shopping for certain ingredients, what to cook when Americans came over for dinner, and how to find certain brand names for an affordable price to be taken as gifts during trips back home.

That was when she tried an English class. It was going as well as it could be expected until the debilitating nausea hit, followed by sleepless nights, diapers, and demanding years of toddlerhood.

Plenty of mothers lived in America without learning English, and they did fine.

Or at least that's what she thought at the time. But here she was, all these years later, still unable to communicate with other parents or her daughters' teachers with ease.

Esma takes another deep breath. Could she do it this time? Could she prove him wrong?

The teacher arrives soon after Esma takes her seat.

Esma tries to pay attention instead of feeling sorry for herself. Luckily, she can understand some of what the teacher is saying.

Instead of towering over them the instructor joins them in the circle of chairs. A retired high school teacher, she asks them to call her by her first name, Meagan. She seems a lot less strict and a lot more friendly than Esma's high school teachers, who certainly never wanted to be called by their first names.

"I am here because I want to give back to my community," Meagan says as she passes everyone a schedule with dates and times and distributes their flimsy—but free—textbooks.

After that, they are paired up to practice introducing themselves to one another. Esma's partner is a woman about the same age as her. Her name is Luna.

This part is easy: the *what's your name, where are you from, how old are you?* basics that Esma learned back in college.

None of those phrases are useful to her now, not in her current predicament.

After the pair-and-share activity, the teacher asks, "Why do you want to learn English?"

"To get a good work," says a young man with a muffled voice.

"To talk with neighbors," says an elderly man with an off-kilter intonation.

"Make friends!" says Luna.

"I want to help my children," Esma adds, carefully sounding the words.

That was a perfectly acceptable response. She gets some nods and smiles from the women around the circle. Other immigrant mothers understood.

She wasn't lying, not exactly. She did want to help her daughters, even if they acted like they didn't need her. At ages thirteen and eight, they already possessed the kind of confidence that Esma forced herself to conjure from thin air.

Besides, her mother had always said, *Think before you speak. There is no need for everyone to know everything.*

Granted, Esma's mother was talking about husbands, or men in general, but her advice—as unorthodox as it might be—applied to many situations: like a classroom for learners of English as a second language.

After all, Esma couldn't have possibly told a room full of strangers that the main reason was that damn vacuum cleaner, could she?

***

Esma gets in line in front of the middle school to pick up her daughter. Nari gets in the car with all her 13-year-old teenage angst.

"Merhaba! How was your day?" Esma says as she tucks Nari's bangs behind her ears. "Let me see your beautiful face."

Nari pulls back. "Not in front of my friends, anne!"

Nari is not in a good mood. Esma longs for the days when all Nari wanted to do was to be with her. Was it easier back then?

Esma's phone rings—it must be the doctor's office. Esma doesn't pick up. She lets them leave a voicemail, then hands the phone to Nari. "Can you tell me what it's about?"

Nari rolls her eyes but still grabs the phone. She turns her body away from Esma and listens to the message while looking out the window. When it's over, Nari puts down Esma's phone in the cup holder between the seats. She is quiet.

Esma can't stand her daughter's silence.

"What is it?" she asks.

"Your appointment is rescheduled for next week. And you need to give blood at the lab beforehand."

Esma sighs. She doesn't like this new doctor at all.

"You could have listened to it yourself," she says. "It's not that difficult. Just try."

Esma's heart sinks. It never ceases to surprise Esma how much Nari sounds like Artan.

Esma forces a smile but keeps her attention on the road. "I am trying. I'm learning so much at my class, aren't I?"

Nari is already distracted with her phone. She types ferociously.

At the next red light, Esma glances at Nari's phone but can't make out the message.

Nari hunches over her backpack and rifles through the contents before producing a piece of paper framed with red and pink hearts. She holds it towards her mom expectantly. "There is a Valentine's party next week at school. Kate's mom will be there. Can you volunteer too?"

For a moment, Nari sounds like her usual child-self. She still needs her mom! How wonderful!

Don't be too eager. "I'd love to. Let me see what else is going on."

Nari crosses her arms. "You always say that. Then you never volunteer. Why can't you be like the other moms?"

Esma thinks about Kate's mom, Lisa—the PTA president. Kate and Nari have been best friends since third grade. Esma enjoys organizing playdates for Nari's friends, and Kate is a wonderful child—curious but respectful. She is always excited to try the snacks Esma brings out but never goes to the fridge without asking for permission.

Lisa, on the other hand, is the opposite. She never takes off her shoes when she comes to pick up Kate. Always in a rush, she turns her nose up if Esma offers her tea or some börek. *Oh, thanks honey*, Lisa always says. Then she'd stare

41

at the evil eye amulet in the entrance and exclaim, *It's wonderful that Kate learns about your culture!* Kate would roll her eyes at her mom while Nari translated.

Whenever Lisa comes by Esma feels like she is on display. But whatever her faults may be, Lisa never fails to show up for her daughter.

Esma turns to Nari and says, "I think I can make it this time."

A quick smile is all Nari offers before she goes back to her cell phone.

Esma turns into the parking lot at the elementary school to pick up Suna. She longs for the days when all her daughters wanted were snacks and cuddles.

***

Esma arrives at Nari's school. After checking in, she walks toward where all the other adults are standing in a circle with Nari by her side. They seem to be talking about sports or maybe a festival? Esma isn't sure. Still, she listens intently and tries to laugh at the appropriate moment.

Finally, Lisa looks up at Esma. Wait, does she not recognize her?

"Hi honey!" Lisa says. "I will be right there with you!"

It must be draining to keep up this flavor of energy.

Nari and Kate find each other and run away giggling. Esma waits at the side of the table, not knowing what to do with her hands. She takes her phone out of her purse and checks her messages. Nothing from her parents.

She sends Artan a quick text: `It's going well! Nari is having a great time.`

Artan responds promptly: `Already? Make sure to get some pictures.`

As if Nari would accept being photographed with her!

"So wonderful! I am so glad that you made it," Lisa says, holding Esma's arm and ushering her inside the group. "Follow me," Lisa tells all the volunteers. She starts walking promptly, leading the way with her ballet flats and green wrap dress. The group leaves behind one or two parents at each corner of the large room. Lisa gives more specific instructions to newcomers while joking with veteran volunteers.

For the next two hours, Esma stands at the juice stand. She is paired with a Greek woman named Iris. Lisa must have thought that they would get along, and it turns out Lisa is right. Esma has a great time. Watching Nari and her classmates dance, giggle, and enjoy themselves is in itself a gift, but making a connection while doing so is even better. At the end of the party, Iris and Esma exchange numbers. Later that night, Iris sends Esma the photos she took of Esma and Nari at the selfie station.

`You two look great,` she texts.

Esma writes back right away: `Thanks! See u soon.`

***

Esma doesn't want to invite her husband and daughters to the graduation ceremony, but in the end, she is left with no choice.

When Suna finds the announcement for the ceremony in her purse, she is so driven that she even recruits Nari to the cause: What should their mom wear? How should she do her hair? What dish should she make for the potluck?

Their excitement makes Esma uncomfortable.

When Esma was growing up, school events were never about things like sea creatures or planets. She never dressed up as her favorite book character or prepared a science exhibit.

No, her school events were about significant historical events—ones that had to be celebrated respectfully and with a serious demeanor. Unlike her daughters' events, which seemed to always celebrate their unique accomplishments, Esma and her classmates were expected to blend in. If there was singing, it was done in a group. If there was a play, it was about collective glory. Rarely did a child stand out, and if someone did, then it was because the teachers wanted to express their dedication to the glory of the nation.

Even so, when Esma was in fifth grade she found herself at the center of the stage because the girl who had originally been cast to recite a nationalist poem—the pretty one with blonde curls that gently sprung as she walked—had gotten sick at the last moment. The play—a reenactment of the War of Independence—was a story about heroic soldiers, backstabbing enemies, and self-sacrificing nurses.

Esma had felt nervous and eager all the time she was on stage. While Esma knew all the lines, she didn't have the self-assurance of the main actress.

After the play was over, her mother had remarked on Esma's performance by saying, "You did well, but I know you are capable of even more."

Esma had hid her sweaty hands behind her back. How did her mom figure out that she forgot a couple of the lines?

***

Esma enters the church's big room with Nari and Suna by her side. Artan is trying to find a parking spot.

It is getting close to Easter, and decorations are already out. An enormous cutout Easter bunny stands next to the entrance. In front is a white basket filled with plastic eggs: pink and blue stripes, purple dots, yellow hearts. More cardboard decorations are set against the wall under an ornamental crucifix.

Around the room some students and their families are already seated. Others, including Luna, are helping to organize the food and beverages on the folding tables in front of the small kitchen area. Cheap plastic sheets cover the tables.

Esma places the tray of chocolate-walnut baklava she made the previous night next to a dozen donuts and some kind of vanilla cake.

She reads the names of other dishes: pastelito, bolani, paska—all look out of place next to the greasy rectangle pizza slices wrapped in Styrofoam and a dozen creamy donuts.

Lisa would have been thrilled to see this cultural diversity!

Her daughters had sat her down about a week ago and provided a list of suggestions. They clearly had discussed the matter of what Esma should bring as if it was a life-and-death situation.

45

"Nothing with eggplant or yogurt," Nari had said seriously.

Suna had suggested, "Maybe we can help you make some baklava? That's always popular!"

Nari had reluctantly approved. "That's good! But we need to make sure people will like it. With walnuts and chocolate, not with pistachio or syrup!"

No self-respecting person would put chocolate in baklava, Esma wanted to say. But Suna and Nari's eager expressions stopped her.

Trying to hide her dread, Esma had acquiesced to their preferences. "That sounds yummy, why don't you two find a recipe that you like?"

At least she got to use her new food processor to grind the walnuts.

Esma turns around and sits in one of the folding chairs arranged in rows facing the stage. Suna sits next to Esma. She is trying to read Nari's texts while Nari exaggerates her annoyance with her little sister. Their playfulness is a rare moment. Esma cherishes it.

The ceremony is a blur. Meagan stands at the podium. She gives a short speech peppered with references to "building community," "a bold journey," and "cultural dialogue." Some people in the audience wipe their tears, while others pretend to pay attention. Then each student goes up to the podium to receive their certificate and to shake the teacher's hand. Some of her classmates throw the certificate in the air. Esma just smiles and waves at her daughters in the audience.

All of it is over in less than twenty minutes.

Esma runs to the restroom before anyone starts to mingle. She holds her wrists under the running cold water to calm herself down, a trick she learned from her father. She takes her phone out to send a text to the family group chat. It would be midnight there now—better to call them tomorrow.

When she comes back into the room, she searches for Artan. How will he congratulate her?

Don't be too eager.

Esma finds Artan immersed in a conversation with Luna. They are in the middle of the room for everyone else to see. Luna is wearing a plain green dress with polka-dots. Her shiny black flats make her look like a middle-aged schoolteacher. The shoes must be new, maybe even bought for this occasion. Luna carefully pulls out each foot to avoid the pain of the blisters on the back of her heels. The tender skin and oozing blood look quite painful, but Luna doesn't seem to mind.

Esma picks up the certificate that's on top of her chair and sits down, then glances up discreetly. Artan is confident and relaxed. He has one hand in his pocket while he uses the other one to articulate whatever points he is trying to make.

Esma wishes she could hear them. Blood rushes to her face. What on earth could they be talking about?

Luna nods with a small head tilt and her bronze curls swirl around the back of her head.

Artan looks interested, energetic, and talkative. The last one hurts the most.

Luna listens intently to Artan. Is she straining to understand? Or is she just drawn to him? Well, she sure is making some friends!

When it's her turn to speak, Luna talks slowly. She hesitates mid-sentence, but keeps going, nevertheless. Looking at her, no one would even guess that her English is flawed. The unfounded confidence is what annoys Esma the most.

The flimsy certificate is wrinkling in her sweaty palms. She unclenches her fist and lays the frail piece of paper on her lap. Her sticky fingers have left a stain at the certificate's corner. No one had even bothered to put the certificates in a proper folder.

She straightens her back and lifts her chin, stands, smooths her skirt, and goes to get some food. The certificate falls from her lap and slides across the church floor.

Esma fills her paper plate with a slice of pizza and a sad-looking salad. They have almost run out of Luna's plate of empanadas as well as Esma's tray of baklava.

She is trying to find a place to sit down when Artan walks over, still carrying the vibrant energy from his conversation.

He says, "Your baklava is very popular. Congratulations! The girls were right after all." He grabs a soda and gets a little bit of everything: chips and salsa, dumplings, falafel, and empanadas nestle together on his plate as if it were a melting pot. He offers her the last empanada. "Don't you want to try some of this? Come on."

Esma responds, "Maybe later, I am not that hungry."

They eat in silence.

***

Esma positions her phone against the paper towel holder and calls her parents around noon. This way they can share

48

a meal despite the time difference. She tells them about the ceremony and how excited the girls were. She makes it into a funny story and makes them laugh about the chocolate-walnut baklava. Her dad wants to know where all the participants are from. He then asks if she plans to take any other classes.

"Didn't you like to do pottery as a child? Maybe you can try that next."

Her mom interrupts her dad. "She is not looking for a new hobby! She is trying to learn English so that she can finally get a job."

"Maybe. I am not sure what I will do yet." She doesn't say *if*.

Her mom says, "Your cousin, remember the one that was your intern back in the day? You should see her new office. She gets paid well too! It's not that difficult, just give it a try."

Esma scowls. "You are right, maybe I can finally start contributing to the household." She can't tell if the screen amplifies or obscures her sarcasm.

***

Esma didn't know what she would do when she headed down to the basement.

As usual, no one is paying attention to Esma, and today she prefers it that way.

Artan is mindlessly watching TV and scrolling on his phone. Suna is asleep, and Nari is probably lying in her bed engrossed in one of her favorite graphic novels.

Esma stands in the middle of the well-organized basement.

49

She walks to the vacuum cleaner and lays it gently on the ground. Her cheeks are flushed. She examines the back of the machine carefully to ascertain its weak spots. Quietly, she walks over to the utility closet and finds the right kind of screwdriver. After she unscrews the back cover, she gently pulls out the cables. She grabs the garden shears from the corner. A sense of relief rushes through her body after she snips the wires.

For a second, she questions what she has done.

After all, she had promised herself.

She had quit.

And she had kept that promise for as long as she could.

She remembers the thrill of her first: the dishwasher. It was another scorching day. Was it August? She had recently given birth to Suna. All summer Esma was stuck inside with a newborn and a four-year-old. The air was humid, the sun heavy, and the baby too little to be near other people. Besides, going anywhere with two children under the age of five was difficult, if not downright impossible.

Esma would stay up late at night to enjoy a moment of solitude and eventually fall asleep as the sun rose, only to be awakened by a crying baby.

One of those mornings, Esma had stepped into the kitchen to find a small puddle of smelly, soapy water on the kitchen floor. This had been happening all summer. Whenever she brought it up, Artan would say, *I'll look into it*, but that day never came.

Esma couldn't wait anymore. As her mother would say, *one trouble was better than a thousand reminders*.

With a decisive turn, Esma had gone to the kids' bedroom. She gave Nari a tablet and put the baby in the playpen. Then she went back to the kitchen and cut up some kitchen towels. She had pulled the dishwasher with all her pent-up anger and put her hand in the back through the small hole on the kitchen counter. She had pulled out the water-disposal tube, shoved the cut-up kitchen towels in it, and shoved everything back in its place. She ran the dishwasher one last time.

Artan was easily convinced when he came home to a flooded kitchen, a disheveled Esma, and two crying children in her arms.

She sets down the shears quietly and reattaches the back of the vacuum cleaner. She pushes the machine back in its place and looks around to make sure that she didn't leave a trace.

She goes back upstairs. Artan is half-asleep on the couch. He jolts up when she sits down.

He pats her hand with his and asks, "Where were you?"

"Just in the basement." She pulls her hand out from under his.

Re-runs of their favorite soap opera are on thanks to international cable.

"Your friend Luna was telling me that she loves this show too," Artan says.

"It's a good show."

For a while they watch the show. The female lead is distraught due to a misunderstanding with her love interest. She waits at the window, batting her eyes, and hoping to catch him before anyone else.

"It is time to get a new vacuum cleaner, this one is beyond repair," Esma says.

"I am sure it's fine. I will look into it tomorrow. You just need the right kind of tools."

"OK, see for yourself."

***

The new vacuum cleaner arrives a couple of weeks later. Esma is drinking her second cup of tea when the bell rings.

Whoever delivers the box disappears by the time Esma opens the door.

Esma looks at the porch, shuts the door behind her, and sits down next to the huge box. It is a crisp morning without a hint of warmth in the air.

That night, as her daughters empty their backpacks and organize their books and homework sheets, Suna brings over the paper with information about the next parent-teacher conference. Esma glances at it, and texts Artan a photo of the page.

    Make sure to ask the teacher about her
    math scores.

Stories at the Kitchen Table

by
Jowan Nabha

The family barbeque is normally a happy event, and today everyone seems to be enjoying themselves—except Zeina. She sits in the kitchen at the house she shares with her husband, Chadi, and his parents and angrily wonders why no one is addressing the elephant in the room. How can they pretend to be a happy family when their family will soon be broken apart forever?

Before the barbeque, Zeina's mother-in-law, Hajje Om Ali, had approached her quietly. "Zeina, there is no need for you to do a thing today. Just relax."

At six months pregnant, Zeina knew her mother-in-law was just looking out for her—especially considering the serious complications she'd had with blood clotting—but Zeina found herself irritated by her words.

Back outside the men work at the makeshift barbeque. Chadi built the grill from old masonry blocks, and it easily fits fifty skewers. As the smell of charcoal embers fills the neighborhood, Zeina is hit with the painful reminder that her husband is not there.

Instead, he's awaiting deportation in a detention center a thousand miles away.

It's been five months. She had just found out she was pregnant with their first child, and they were both excited for the future. A future that may now never come to be.

A sudden change in the breeze sends smoke through the screen door and Zeina coughs. She moves to a more secluded part of the kitchen and watches her mother-in-law and sisters-in-law prepare side dishes. They're immersed in laughing conversation and occasionally glance over at Zeina.

"Zeina, come take a small bite for me, dear." Hajje Om Ali reaches over with a piece of bread wrapped in kibbee nayee and some veggies.

Zeina's blood boils. She slams her fists on the kitchen table and stands. "What is wrong with you? Have you all gone completely mad?"

Everyone stops what they are doing.

Zeina looks around and steps away from the table. "Why are you all acting like everything is normal? As if we don't have a huge catastrophe on our hands? I can't believe I almost bought into this charade."

"Try to calm down," says Amal, Zeina's oldest sister-in-law. "You don't want anything to happen to the baby, now do you? We are trying our best with what we know, but your outburst does not help. This is just your hormones talking."

"My outburst doesn't help? I cannot believe you people. My husband, my amazing husband Chadi...." Zeina starts to sob. "He could be deported any day, and yet I'm supposed to sit around, sample kibbee nayee, and act as if my world may not be falling apart within days? Do you know how delusional you sound?"

"This is not in our hands anymore," Amal says, her voice calm although she's clearly growing annoyed. "We cannot dwell on things that Allah has taken out of our control. Our decision to have this family dinner is to bring us closer, not to divide us any further. Chadi is always in our prayers and duaa. You have no idea how hard it is for us to deal with his departure. But what can we do other than what has already been attempted?"

Zeina slowly sits back down and lays her head on the table, continuing to cry. Her life is imploding right in front of her eyes, and there's nothing she can do about it? Their child will come into this world unsure if their father will ever be a part of their life.

"Pick up your head, girl, and quit your whining."

Zeina looks up. "Hajje?"

Hajje Om Ali sniffs. "How dare you sit there blaming us for attempting to live some type of normalcy while you are the one to blame for Chadi being in this position to begin with."

Stunned, Zeina doesn't speak.

"He was never home," Hajje Om Ali continues. "He worked day and night to try to provide a life for you that he could not keep up with. Your lifestyle ruined him. It led him to crime, and that's why he faces deportation. He was safe. He was content with the life we live. *You* ruined him." Hajje jabs her finger accusingly at Zeina.

Without a word, Zeina gets up and runs to her room. She shuts the door and plops onto the bed, tears muffled by her pillow.

How can her in-laws believe she's the reason Chadi will be deported? She never asked him to commit crimes for her. She would've been happy as long as he was by her side.

Suddenly Zeina can't spend another second in this house, but she knows she can't leave quite yet, not without making another scene. She packs essentials in a small suitcase, including clothes, medicine, and cash Chadi had saved up for them that ICE had not confiscated. There would be enough for her to make it on her own for a short while, but she'd need to find a job. It would be difficult, but Zeina knows she's making the right choice for her and her baby.

She waits until the guests leave and her in-laws are fast asleep. Her mother-in-law had not come in to check on her or say goodnight as she usually would. In fact, nobody had acknowledged her at all, which Zeina found better since she could not stand to see any of their faces.

Zeina calls a taxi, and within fifteen minutes she opens her front door for the last time. This will be the fresh start she needs. She can focus on helping Chadi come home and on raising her baby without constantly feeling the hate and resentment from her in-laws.

Before closing the front door, Zeina looks back at the kitchen table, remembering all the happy dinners and family moments she shared with Chadi. The kitchen table that holds so many beautiful memories is also where her whole world came crashing down, but now it's time to find another place where those beautiful memories can become possible once more.

She closes the door and steps into her new future.

Honest Hummus in the Red Tubberware

by
Koloud Fawzi Omar Abdul Aziz Tarapolsi

For as long as I can remember, I have never gone without enjoying hummus weekly. My mother used to lovingly make it for me—waiting fresh on the prestigious top shelf of the fridge inside a red tubberware container—but since I'm away, I've been making my own.

I can never seem to recall when I first learned how to make this humble dish. Also lost from my memory is any recollection of when exactly I was taught to put my full essence into cooking, to give it *nafas*, a breath. Once I conquered cooking with nafas I didn't need to follow the exact rules, because every dish always came out delicious.

On Fridays I shop for dehydrated chickpeas at the organic corner market near my closet-sized grad school apartment; the smallest so far, with the one window counter that serves as my thesis desk, a food preparation station, and a nightstand.

Technically, I don't need organic chickpeas, which the market likes to refer to as garbanzo beans in ginormous childlike letters on the chalkboard sign. I'll never quite understand why the heavenly balls in the oversized white bins—on the right side of aisle 12—need an alias, as if a code name might turn them into a double agent.

I like coming here because of the clear-lidded bins. They remind me a little of being home and weighing exactly the food I need instead of having my goods presented in predetermined, stacked receptacles, hidden inside an endless, mega grocery store labyrinth. I bring my own empty container and fill it to just before the lip, making sure to leave room for the exhilaration of ululations.

My container is blue, tall, and exactly 4.5 ounces. After I fill it with the little golden balls of joy, the cashier Sandy weighs it at the counter and takes the 4.5 ounces off the bill. Another reason I like coming here: They are honest.

Sandy reminds me that the market encourages everyone to now bring in their own bags and packaging. I obediently smile and nod. I wasn't sure if Sandy would understand that people around the world have been doing that for centuries. I also don't want to take away her proud ownership of parroting the words "reduce, reuse, recycle" in the correct order like the poster behind her screams in massive, white upper-case letters on a green background.

Chickpeas should be carried home in something familiar to welcome them, my mother likes to say. For years she's been using the same burlap sacks for her souk trips. I look forward to my week ending with the sound of my chickpeas vaulting off the blue lid as I bounce up the stairs to my apartment.

In my kitchen, chickpeas have their own bowl for soaking. It has no obligation in this world other than to give the beautiful, beige, delectable beads a deep, freshwater bath. I swirl every perfect, hard nugget as they dance between my fingers. I can almost hear giggles as they joust and scuffle over the best spots in their bowl. After a few hours the water grows murky from the chickpeas' wearisome farm voyage, so I carefully cradle the edge as I tip the lathed wooden bowl over the sink to release the darkness down the drain. One or two chickpeas might attempt to show off with a fancy tuck position dive, but I gently pick them up and return them to their applauding fans along with new, refreshingly crisp, pristine bath water.

On Saturday mornings I slip on my Bluetooth hat and play Farid al-Atrash at top volume on my phone. Specifically, his romantic songs since it's been scientifically proven chickpeas do not appreciate hearing me echo his political or religious songs. I learned my lesson when I conducted the research myself after he and I accidentally engaged in a non-gooeyness encrusted refrain. That haunting incident occurred in my fourth college apartment—the last one to have an actual eating table.

At some point, when Farid provides our voices a reprieve to play his eleven-string musical instrument, I drain the softened chickpeas and let them rest in a colander to observe my impressive air oud skills. After a few minutes— or half an hour, as I tend to lose track of time when I am in the zone—I add fresh water to a pot. I include baking soda and gently place the relaxed legumes at the bottom to await the boiling party getting underway.

After a couple of hours, I switch to Um Kalthoum, since the chickpeas like to rest with a velvety ballad after the boiling water tumbling gymnastics they have performed. Before anything else, they insist on getting undressed as they've worked up quite a sweat. I sit facing my one window counter and remove the translucent jackets off each single garbanzo, as the Queen of Love Songs' voice and mine mix with what I can only imagine are sighs of relief as they go nude.

In the olden, traditional days, my grandmother—allahyarhamha—scooped out handfuls of the naked, tranquil morsels to smash them with spices with a mortar and pestle. She started stories with "kan ya makan" and ended them with far-off, exotic lands full of natives, white as waves, who ground the dried chickpeas as flour and even coffee. It was only years later after she'd passed on that I learned that, despite her tales beginning with "once upon a time," they were saturated with the truth.

Nowadays I pull out my trusty, dented electric food processor, which still runs great despite all the battle scars from surviving too many moving boxes. I insert the blissful chickpeas, handmade tahini, freshly squeezed lemon juice, olive oil, four cloves of garlic—my mother likes to say any less is someone being cheap—and a pinch of sea salt and cumin. It never matters the order, but it does matter how long. Everything needs time to mingle and anyone who takes them out in fewer than seven minutes should be arrested. Yes, I hear the politicians complain our jails are full, but not taking the time to get this right should be taken seriously as it would be a true hummuscide.

I add a few ice cubes and let the processor cool to not get too hot and bothered during those seven plus minutes. Once the texture is light as air, I scrape a little into a single bowl to enjoy a warm, savory spread with extra olive oil. The stout, pungent smell of garlic quickly fills the atmosphere of my miniscule apartment and breathes life into my senses.

I place the rest of the healthy, nourishing snack in the red tubberware. I still remember the first time my mother snuck it into my suitcase, stuffed with cookies that smelled like hummus when I ate them alone in my first campus dorm.

The cookies grew salty from my tears as I longed for the comforting smells of familiarity.

The red tubberware will stay in the fridge till it is empty on Thursday. All week I will add the hummus bi tahini as a side to my breakfast eggs, or place a big dollop on my lunch sandwich, or warm up a bowl to drizzle on grilled lamb for dinner. It is also perfect to pull out when an unexpected guest or two stops by to share stories and celebrate time together. This, of course, happens after they politely refuse the food two times while I thrice vehemently insist.

Once a coworker at my library work study brought hummus from a store in a cold, clear plastic container. It did not look like a tubberware that had been tossed in the dishwasher a billion gazillion times. Or one banged around in a homebound suitcase by customs officials who also couldn't pronounce the P when they demanded to know what was inside.

The coworker did not like that I was honest when I said it was not real hummus bi tahini. They stabbed their finger at the lid in an effort to convince me. I looked at the capital letters which spelled hummus in orange as they pointed at the olive and what appeared to be a poison ivy sprig that were obviously not inside.

"I think in America they call this false advertising," I whispered, but the coworker didn't buy it.

"Honest hummus starts by being welcomed in your home," I added, as if it might mean something.

But the coworker was not interested in honest hummus.

"Foodie," they mumbled under their breath like it was a dirty word. They rolled their eyes and turned to flirt with the blonde in New Arrivals.

Honest hummus made by hand at home tastes like love,
I wanted to add.

I could still say it…but I didn't.

They wouldn't understand nafas.

The Middle Ground

by
Malack Jallad

1...2...3 Hands
1...2...3 Mouth
1...2...3 Nose
1...2...3 *Where was I?*
1...2...3 Hands
1...2...3 Mouth
1... *Did I rinse my mouth three times?*
Again
1...2...3 Hands
1...2...3 Mouth
1...2...3 Nose
1...2...3 Face
1...2...3 Arms
1...2...*The water didn't reach above the elbow, did it?*
1...2...3 Hands
1...2...3 Mouth
1...2...3 Nose
1...2...3 Face
1...2...3 Arms
1...2...3 Head
1...2...3 Neck
1...2...3 Ears
1...2...3 Feet
But my feet hit the ground,
Again.

The sound of the *Adhan* was long gone by the time I prayed.
And even then, I could barely utter God's words without feeling the need to restart.
And so I did.
Again.
And again.

Before long I could hear the birds outside.
The next prayer was near.
I would need to do it all again.
5 times over.

The Prophet preached *Alaietidal*.
Yet I preach irrationality.

Moderation is but the medium between two extremes.
The gray area
The middle ground
But where does one find it?
And really, why can't I?

My entire life I have tried to practice what he preached,
Yet I am a victim of my own hypocrisy.
So here I remain.
Alone.

But I don't like the word "alone," for God is always with me.
Yet sometimes I feel it is not that simple.
Life is meant to be simple.
In its simplicity, temperance exists.
Does it not?
Yet here I remain.

1…2…3…

THE

"*Ja-nin?*"
"Here!"
"Did I pronounce that correctly?"
"It's Jenin, pronounced *Je-neen*, but close enough!"

I hope my voice didn't sound too high pitched.
Or that I didn't look too startled when my pen fell to the
floor.

I wish I could add exclamation points to my conversations
IRL.
Or click on "like" to end them.
Or maybe even just talk through emojis.

I love talking, but the first day of class will forever make me
nervous.
I never know what to say.

I hate ice breakers.
There is nothing interesting about me.
I don't have any fun facts,
Or at least ones that my class would enjoy.

Why are icebreakers even a thing?
I already feel that I am on thin ice.
Or that perhaps this is just the tip of the iceberg.

My name is Jenin.
Named after the city of Jenin, Palestine,
Where both my parents are from.
I guess Jenin rhymes with *Falesteen*.
Maybe I should say that.

I wear a gold necklace with my name in Arabic every day.
An Arab girl staple.
Siti brought it back with her from Palestine.
How I long to visit my homeland.
My homeland?

Because beyond the gold necklace with my name in Arabic
I do not feel Arab enough.
Beyond the *keffiyeh* I often wear on top my *hijab*
I do not feel Arab enough.
And beyond the flag that hangs in my room,
the protests I've attended,
and the DNA I carry
I am not Arab enough.

Yet, I am not American either.

Too Arab to feel American and too American to feel Arab.
Where is the middle ground?
That is the question.

I sometimes feel like a fake Arab.
An imposter amongst my own
Like the *thobe* I wear is nothing more than dress-up.

Ana dammi falastini more like my blood boils at the thought of forgetting how to speak my first language.

Palestine bleeds with every broken Arabic word that comes out of my mouth.
Is this pain to my mother tongue a constant reminder of my lack of connection to my homeland?
Is this the middle ground?

Because here I am living in the same country that aids in the killing of mine
Where my American passport is a so-called privilege, a protection
Yet my Palestinian *Haweeya* refuses me access to Jerusalem.

Where is the middle ground?

"Can you please share a fun fact about yourself?"

What can I say?
I don't have much time to think
Let alone overthink
Too many things

Should I speak of the moral conflict
That keeps me up at night?
But how can I do so without going on a tangent
About Palestinian rights?

Because it's not a conflict, I would explain
A conflict constitutes equal footing
Not guns versus rocks.

But you see that's the thing
Icebreakers are meant to be about yourself
About me
But how can I speak of me without speaking of them
Of my people
Yet I cannot make their struggles my own?

How can I explain without acknowledgement,
And how can I acknowledge without explanation?

I can't.

Because it feels that a body of water is not the only thing
keeping us apart.

*"Hello everyone, my name is Jenin and a fun fact about me
is that…."*

MIDDLE

Siti stands between the fence
At the corner of diligence and nonchalance
Hidden except for a single sign
No trespassing
No one beyond

I am on the fence about joining
But this isn't the first time
Random parking lot
Luscious grape leaves
Why wouldn't I?

She clutches the plastic grocery bag
Prepped with nothing but her frail hands
As she carefully picks the leaves
Stem by stem
Hand by hand

There must be a science to picking grape leaves
Search green and wide
Pull, but not too hard
Cut at the stem, but not too close
Or they won't last

It is a sight that never fails to amaze me
For I can never understand

Is there some kind of genetic predisposition to this
knowledge
One that I wouldn't know of
Because in the eyes of America
I am not of Arab descent

For that, I must not be enough

I can never be like her
Because even beyond her aging eyes
Siti is like a surgeon
Her technique evidently precise

She's delicate yet stern on her bearing
Articulate yet confident in her work
Something I can never be

I find comfort in her confidence
For I often question mine
She doesn't have any questions
As do I

What if I pick them wrong?
What if I do it wrong?
What if I am wrong?

I will never understand

She stands next to the collection of leaves turned garbage
bag
Smiling at her trophy
A prized possession amongst the women of the land

We lay them out in piles she judged by size
And then stuff them with eyed grains of rice
Wrap them in aluminum covering

Siti then begins the cooking process
Porcelain plate placed on top of the *tunjara*
Eyeing every ingredient

They say you cannot ask an Arab woman for a recipe
For the eye is the greatest ingredient
There perhaps exists no authentic cookbooks written by us
As we tend to as we see it

Am I *us*?
Because I don't seem to have an eye for such tending

Is it because I sought definition and not the lack thereof?
Discrete measurements of ingredients, step by step
instruction, stability somewhat
Is this why I now seek concrete answers to the million
questions of life?

Is *not knowing* the premise of my greatest anxieties
One that would haunt me beyond my formative years?

Or is it because I refused to learn to cook early on
Was I unconsciously breaking the gender norms I grew up
accustomed to
Because looking back I was never fond of such duties
inclined to women
Of duties
A victim to
A witness to
Expected of *us*

Yet as I savor the sour delicacy of my grandmother's
cooking
I feel that I leave a sour taste on my mother tongue
For this innate refusal to learn to cook
Perhaps it's synonymous to myself
Perhaps like precious leaves it stems beyond

But I remain
As I always do
Conversing through smiles and nods
For they say food is the universal language
So maybe then I can be understood this way

As Palestine bleeds with every broken word I utter
Siti sutures
So even for a little while
I can feel connected

But then again I still remain conflicted

For the eyes can be deceiving
And so can I

GROUND

Hunched backs on the airport floor
Bags of gifts that we could barely afford
And yet here we are on our way

The suitcase and I let out a collective sigh when my mother
unzipped it
Its lungs seemed to expand as mine constricted
For I felt all eyes on me

Three pounds over the weight limit
Stuffed with whatever we could fit into it
Palestine here we come

As we board the plane, the air is heavy
Hours early but last to board
Your typical Arab family
Always late
With exception to the airport

All eyes on us as we sought our seats
Annoying looks at the crying child in my arms
A cousin 20 years my junior

A woman softly cries in the corner
"I'm sure their bags were checked,"
Her mother reassures her

We would return the same way we departed
Except this time another bag full
Zaatar and cheese and *Mansaf* spices
Olives from *Siti*'s tree
Goodies from back home

We won't find them here
Not in this home

But which do I call home?

Edible souvenirs
Or reminders of a time before us
I do not know

Tangible memories
For experiences I will not forget
That I do know

These experiences now unfaze me
Too many to list

Airports and parks and large families
Never being on time
Chaos ensues where we reside

Pronouncing English words wrong
For there is no letter P in Arabic

The tendencies of the immigrant parent
And the eldest daughter phenomenon

And the best of food

Cannot forget about the latter

Not one original experience or thought

Collective experiences or stereotypes
Where is the middle ground?

They no longer faze me
These experiences or whatever they may be
But perhaps they never did
For most of my life I've been oblivious

As this was all I knew

Is it weird to experience cultural shock
While living in the same place you grew up in?

Because as I grow older I learn
And I question
And I continue to be hit with the weight of realization

The middle ground sinks in
Amidst the contemplation
And I am left on its edge

Because I feel grateful to have been raised the way I was
Amongst the beauty of culture
But these constant realizations
Sudden as they are
Make me wonder

Is there perhaps more to what I know
A result of well-hidden problems
Of unresolved trauma
Sheltered was I

Do I just want to feel connected
Part of a whole
Even if it means
Staying in oblivion

That's not like me though
Consciously that is

But I cannot pick and choose
Can I?

It is never ending
This moral conflict
Two extremes
Me

And so what do I do?

I suppose I tend to just tread lightly
With nothing but humor to cope

I should write a book actually
Inside Jokes for the Child of an Immigrant
Because maybe then I won't forget them

Jokes we use as coping mechanisms
Behind their words,
complexity and buried generational trauma
Yet a sense of comfort remains within them
Even if my own children will never understand them

Jokes based on our experiences
And of those before us
Jokes of love and indifference
For they were once children too

But they were children without choices
Unlike us

Perhaps then this moral conflict is passed on
Inherited by those that come after
But who bears the brunt
And who bears the fruit of its labor
I don't know the answer

Because now we are left with this ultimate responsibility
To make these choices

What to keep and what to pass on
What to cling to and what to leave
Break generational curses
while also cultivate appreciation for our culture
Eradicate the stigma but fix our representation

Embrace your roots in the land where they are not watered
Because only then you can grow

Hold onto your culture like it's no other
But continue to tread lightly
Or else

1…2…3…Inhale

1…2…3…Exhale

"It's all in your head."

1…2…3…Sleep

1…2…3…Recite

God does not burden a soul beyond that it could bear

One Hundred Proverbs

by
Koloud Fawzi Omar Abdul Aziz Tarapolsi

درنة إلى الإسكندرية

Yusuf gave his sons the broken promise as if delivered on a feather tray, ready to take flight.

"Of course I'll be back, Inshallah, of course."

"When?" Salih's cracked voice carried the weight of the question.

"As soon as the Colonizers are out I'll be back for you. We'll all return home. Inshallah."

Yusuf avoided his sons' eyes in the moonlight.

It's been seven days since they left their village together.

They traveled at night so no one could see them, with their Kouloughlis guide keeping them close together as there was safety in numbers.

The five fathers, their nine young sons plus guide all bent themselves against the hot, dry winds in the singular parade of bodies. With their bent frames and burlap sacks, they looked like a two-legged caravan of camels. The fathers were cautious of other travelers who may rob them. Warned by their taitas, the sons were thinking of djinns who could appear in either human or animal form.

Ahead of Yusuf, Salih limped across the rugged ground in silence without complaint. Yusuf's heart ached to see his son so small, yet so stoic in the face of suffering.

"Salih."

His son looked back at him, his dark handed-down turban too large to fit around his head. His eyes shone bright in a moonbeam.

"Baba?"

"Let's rest a moment. We will catch up with the others."

Fethi, his oldest, stopped alongside his brother. His jarid dragged, despite being tied around both tiny shoulders. Yusuf joined them, untying his prayer rug for them to sit while he helped them remove their leather boots. Despite their sirwal diligently tucked into the tops of their boots, the endless sand and pebbles worked their way inside, and Yusuf squeezed the worn-out hard heel of Salih's boot at the sight of his child's bloodied and blistered feet. In his heart he cursed the Colonizers, raged at the awful necessity of fleeing Libya to cross desert, coast, and rocky badlands to Türkiye, but if his young sons could be so restrained with blistered feet and parched lips, he needed to do the same.

"Do you think I will finally sleep at the orphanage?" Salih winced as he pulled up his boots. "Or will the djinns that appear in the sky still follow us there?"

"I have not seen them since we left our home. They seem to only appear over our skies." Yusuf could not explain how the metal machines floated in the air but was grateful he no longer heard their annoying grinding sound. "For now, let us catch up to the others."

The others included Yusuf's cousin Ali, along with his boys Majid and Omar, and Cousin Mustafa with his twins Aziz and Tariq. Then there was also Yusuf's neighbor Amir with his sons Mohammed and Osama, and his other neighbor Mahmoud with his only son Yahya.

"We can't get too close to the sea, or the fishermen might see us," their guide uttered in a low voice as he pointed toward the water on their first night.

Sand dunes dominated the landscape. They had passed the Frontier Wall a few nights ago, the shiny barbed wire glistened in the desert moonlight, but their guide knew of an area that had recently been cut for passage and they had gone through safely. The patrol tanks and djinns in the sky somehow missed their crossing. Some days the group traveled close to the coast. In the dark of night, they heard the waves breaking and smelt the perfume of salt and fish.

Yusuf and the other fathers' dark turbans rotated around their foreheads and black shashiyah a few times, then swept down to cover their mouths against the dust that raged through the night air. The older men's jarids were tailor-made for them by the women in the village. They fit perfectly wrapped around their bodies and tied over the right shoulder. But some of the younger boys did not fit theirs. Instead of the outer cloak ending around their heads like their fathers, most were wrapped around their small bodies twice and tied on both shoulders.

Their guide used the stars to navigate through the steep, sandy terrain. His family were known travel guides, and he grew up reading the night sky and memorizing the safe houses that took in weary travelers. He pulled out two threads, one white, one black, and looked at them against the horizon.

"We will stop here," he whispered to the first person behind him, and his instructions went down the line to the others.

84

The sky was streaked a light pink by the time they found the large oasis. Fethi untied prayer rugs from the top of Yusuf's bag—the boys' bags only held food and water, as the rugs were too heavy for them. The other older boys rolled out rugs for themselves and their fathers. Yusuf watched as Salih helped the young Yahya with his father's bag. Mahmoud was collecting palm tree branches to use as cover. The group used sand for their wudu and then performed their prayers, led by Mohammed, the oldest boy. Afterwards, they sat in a circle so a father could share a proverb.

Each of the five fathers had shared one proverb each day after prayers to help distract the boys from the seemingly endless trip. At night they took turns collecting firewood and starting the cooking fire while the boys gathered the rugs in a circle to listen. The fathers hoped the proverbs would allow them to pass on the wisdom from their own elders.

"The night with its ears and the day with its eyes," Ali whispered. "Every sound is magnified in the stillness of the night. Always use caution equally when the sun has set, even when there is no danger that you fear in the moonlight."

"But we are too far to be heard, how can anyone see us in the dark?" Salih asked.

Yusuf caught the guide's smile. He must be used to Salih's endless inquiry each time anyone spoke.

"The fishermen we saw earlier are on the water for hours with nothing to do but stare at the sea and beach. They see all shadows that should not be there." Ali answered.

Ali made each of the boys repeat the proverb before the next father shared his. Their voices each echoed "الليل بوذيناته والنهار بعويناته" in the desert dusk, the hot air sticking their words together like grains of cooked rice.

Tomorrow they would reach al-Iskandariyah, and their guide had promised them a safe house with a fellahin he knew. The traveling group could sleep during the day without worry while the guide looked for a boat to take them across al-Nil. There were low areas where they could cross by foot, but the crocodiles made it too dangerous.

Yusuf was not too concerned with the water passage since their guide had assured them he had traveled on this path many times before. Yusuf could not shake the feeling that maybe he should have trusted his sons with his cousins while he stayed behind to protect the village.

الجبل الأخضر

Salwa and Um Yusuf enter the masjid through the side door, and a woman inside immediately ushers them through to another door. Her eyes take a moment to adjust to the darkness as she discerns the outlines of the other mothers in the village. She sets the baby down in the corner with the other toddlers to play.

"Alhamdillah, Um Fethi and Um Yusuf are finally here," Moufida's voice whispers from underneath the closed window shutters.

"Salam alakum, my apologies, Um Mohamed. The goat escaped and it took all of us to catch it." Salwa gathers her haik around her body to sit down next to Um Yusuf. The layers of cloth add extra cushion as she settles in the circle.

"We have not started, so you have not missed anything." Moufida's voice carries to the back of the room. "We need to decide which of our men will be carrying which items. There is no need for all of them to take a cooking pot. One of the men will carry the pot, another will take spices, and so forth."

"I will be happy to provide all the spices from my garden," Salwa says.

"The guide our sheiks found has assured us that there will be plenty of game for the men to catch, so we should not give them too much of our meat. We need to send that to our men that are fighting," Um Yahya adds. There are new worry lines mingling with her forehead tattoo lines since the last time Salwa saw her. Salwa wonders if they are due to her worrying for her son Yahya, who at eight is the youngest in the group.

"Our men will have plenty to eat, I am not worried about them." Moufida adds. Her son Mohammed is fourteen and will be one of the oldest boys on the journey. He is very talented with a sling and hunts the local ibex with ease.

The women in the room start to make a list of all the items the men will need and take an inventory of the clothes they will have to gather.

"Since they are traveling in the desert, the group would need beige jarids. The white ones might be detected from the sky djinns the Colonizers fly." Um Aziz reminds everyone of the strange objects that had given her twins nightmares. "We will have to store their white jarids for future, happier occasions, Inshallah."

While the rest of the women continue with their list of the outer cloaks that had inspired the toga, Salwa thinks of all the men and boys that had been killed by the Colonizers in the nine years since the second Italo-Senussi war had started. She knows in her head that sending her sons on this journey is the only way to save their lives, but her heart cannot bear the loss.

Salih had only been a toddler when news of the Colonizers first arriving had reached their village. Salwa remembers carrying him to the upper fields, tied to her back as he had gotten too heavy for her hip. Now he was old enough to walk across hundreds of kilometers, just as his baby sister was reaching the same age.

Um Yusuf reaches out her hand and places it on Salwa's knee. "The fathers will take care of the boys," she assures her, "and we will endure the extra work on our farms and protect each other until the men's safe return."

درنة إلى يَافَا

Yusuf took the extra wool farmla off Salih and draped it over his arm. Fethi's farmla was already on the other arm. Sweat soaked down both boys' backs. After fifteen days, the desert sand had turned to shrublands that provided an occasional break from the grueling night winds off the coast. They made sure to always stay together since the howling of the golden jackals scared the younger boys. They believed the sky djinns had followed them and shape-shifted into a new terror.

"How much farther?" Salih inquired for the third time that night.

"Inshallah, only a few more days," the guide said.

The terrain was unpredictable as none of the men on the trip had ever traveled this far before, except for their guide. The guide was something the men agreed they would pool their money for once the village elder sheiks outlined the trip to save their sons. They all knew of the fate that would befall them once the Colonizers spread into the upper mountain villages if they did nothing.

It was hot as they moved through the olive groves, but once they reached the cool mountain air later in their journey they would need the extra layers. Mustafa had extra leather in his bag and had already replaced several hole-ridden, worn-out bottoms of the boys' shoes.

Yusuf looked at his sons and tried to imagine returning to a time when they would be together. He worried if his boys would remember the spot where their mother grew mint, the cuts in the wood grain of the table they sliced meat on, or their friends' smiling faces at the masjid's Eid and Mawlid celebrations. Salih was always the first one awake when he heard the beat of the drums and clang of the cymbals approach to announce Mawlid. He would run to his parents' room first to make sure they woke up in time to see the procession pass their farmhouse. The vibrations, noise, and dry throats from all the men singing praises to their prophet would last well into the night in the masjid garden his mother helped maintain.

Yusuf remembered the first Mawlid with Salwa as his wife, her belly heavy with Fethi. He had returned home from the masjid full of happiness and had hugged Salwa for too long. As she giggled and tried to get away, he whispered in her ear, "I will buy you the fastest horse in the land so you can ride free."

Yusuf held onto the memory as he watched his sons sprint ahead without their heavy farmla. Yusuf slowed to be with a few of the other men. He listened as they discussed how to rid their homeland of the Colonizers.

"As soon as I get back, Inshallah, I will take up arms," Ali said to the rest of the men.

"Yes, I have mine ready, buried in the backyard next to the chickens. I left my wife with her father, and he knows how to use it," Mustafa shared.

Yusuf's neighbor Amir clenched his fists. "Those sons of bitches better not come looking for my sons while my wife is alone. My cousin is next door, but he has his own wife and daughters to protect."

They stopped for the daybreak on the outskirts of a pistachio farm. The men and boys quickly performed their prayers and gathered for proverbs before sleep. The mild sweet smell filled the air around their tight circle.

Mahmoud started with the proverb, "He who is patient obtains."

"Obtains what?" Salih asked his father.

"It does not matter what will be obtained, it matters more that you will be rewarded for having patience," Yusuf explained.

But the boys only thought of the reward of returning home. The sadness in their hearts deepened with each incremental step towards their destination. Yusuf and his sons were not looking forward to being split from each other.

All the boys repeated "اللّي يصبر ينال" after each other.

Yusuf tugged on his beard and thought of Salwa at home, alone with the baby. He now wished he had also left her with a gun, instead of bringing it with him.

الجبل الأخضر

Salwa fills the bags to the brim.

She can't stop her tears as she slices the dried meats, pits the dates, and shells the nuts. She packs it all in small pouches. The women of the village had gathered together to work on dehydrating spices in her kitchen, but now they are all gone. She inserts a pouch of spices into all three bags. In a second pouch, which she will only add to her sons' bags, she includes dirt and a few mint roots from her garden. She had cut and sewn the pouches from the baby's first outfit. Salwa prays her sons will not forget the familiarity of their sister.

Salwa's long, dark hair is plaited in a single braid, but loose strands hang over her eyes. Their journey will take weeks. The guide has warned they will have to travel at night, and it will be dangerous. She wants to make sure they never go without her spices. Salwa brushes her hair away from her tear-streaked face and continues to stack everything within the bags until she can add no more.

Once she finishes with the bags, Salwa brings Yusuf's old clothes to work on the last of the hemming by the fire while the bread bakes in the corner stone stove. She moves the candle off the shelf and puts it closer to her on the one lone, low table in the room. The light flickers before settling down.

Salwa has to take in Yusuf's old sadriay quite a bit to fit Salih, who does not share the same broad shoulders as his father and brother. She removes the extra buttons on the front and adds them to a compartment to be hemmed later when they are needed. The black silk on the vest is heavily knitted and takes extra time to fold under. Instead of cutting off the extra fabric, Salwa adds extra socks before hand-sewing the fold closed. In the rolled-up sleeves of their long, white qamis she slips in extra underwear. Finally, she hems the sirwals but does not add anything in the folds. Since the ends will be tucked into the boys' leather boots, anything she places there might become too dirty.

Salih is tall for his age, so the boys are often mistaken for twins, but they were born eleven months apart. While they both have dark hair and a number of features similar to Yusuf, they carry their mother's smile and her kind eyes.

Yusuf and the boys sleep as Salwa hems. Yusuf is restless in his sleep, and Salwa wonders if he is dreaming about leaving for the orphanage in the morning. Yusuf's mother, Amal, also lives with them but her bed is empty as she is away in the next village helping Yusuf's sister, who has recently lost her husband. Amal had left the morning after the masjid meeting when she heard the news.

The baby coos at her feet while Salwa sews and sits by the morning bread fire, flipping the round, delicious discs when needed. The darkness outside hangs over their impending departure and adds an extra layer of sorrow to Salwa's heart. She hums softly to the baby in the hope she would not sense her mother's sadness and start to cry.

Traveling in the summer will be extra difficult with the heat, but Salwa and Yusuf know they have no choice. If the boys stayed, there would be no opportunities for them, no prospects. Their only other option was to hide in the mountains behind the village and spend their time worrying about being found. They would have to continuously shift camps while praying they remain undiscovered so no poisonous gases would be unleashed upon them.

No, the men had to take their sons out of the country, or they would be killed by the Colonizers.

At first Salwa was unsure what to think about the light-skinned men that suddenly appeared on the shores of her home and claimed ancestral ownership of her homeland. The collapsing ruins in the desert had been built by their grandparents' grandparents and proved they had been there before. At first, everyone had been happy the Colonizers had rid them of the Ottoman overlords.

Soon the Colonizers built new roads and cathedrals of imported marble that had to be carried off of ships on the bent backs of locals. Next, they created taxes and laws to regulate their newfound and abundant colony. The Colonizers wanted to destroy the local language and culture. They proceeded to replace it with their own so that the settlers they brought in felt at home. Salwa did not understand how they could claim to be a superior race yet had not been able to find happiness in their own country.

Every day came more bad news from the Capital reached Jabel al-Akhdar of vicious home invasions and lynchings on street corners. Moufida's husband, Amir, had told them that the Colonizers would leave the bodies hanging from the gallows in the public square for three days so that they were seen by everyone, especially the children. When the locals pleaded that they needed to cleanse the bodies within twenty-four hours the Colonizers only laughed. There is an utter cruelty served with a side of entitlement that allows them to regard anyone who is not a white male as only existing to serve them. Afterwards, they are expendable. Salwa overheard the imam at the souk say that while the Colonizers had been smiling, hand-shaking signers at the first Geneva Convention, they willfully ignored the treaty in their treatment of real humans.

A new law was announced that demanded that all boys who lived in the Capital between the ages of ten and twenty-five must come to the Headquarters to register. The news came one day by way of a freckle-faced Colonizer in an oversized light tan suit, who stood outside the masjid doorstep to read the Pacification Decree. His long sleeves nearly covered his hands as he held the official-looking paper. His Arabic was loud and came with too many cruel spoken, classical words that some locals needed to have translated into colloquial Arabic. Salwa remembers Yusuf laughing as he told her about the interpreter the Colonizers had sent who needed an interpreter.

The families that lived in the Capital took their sons obediently to the new headquarters erected of marble. Many went because they were curious about the new building material that was far more exotic than the mud homes they lived in. There were even rumors it had a toilet inside. But none of their sons were ever seen again after they entered the multi-level stone structure with its grand arches. Salwa and Yusuf did not wait for that law to be announced in their village of Jabel al-Akhdar.

درنة إلى بيروت

"The water we passed today reminds me of another proverb." Mustafa's words echoed on the cave walls. Their guide told them they were somewhere outside of Bayrut.

"Don't throw stones in the well you drink from," Mustafa said. "Consider your community, your family, and your friends when you know your actions will bring more than just harm to yourself. Wrong doings not only affect the health, mental or physical, but also the happiness of others close to you."

Yusuf tugs on his beard as he listens.

"But we will not be with our community," Aziz, one of Mustafa's twin boys, said. His brother Tariq sat close by and nodded his own head in agreement.

"Yes, but you carry your father's name everywhere you go. Your community will always be with you. Now let's memorize it: "البير الَّلي تشرب منه ماترمي فيه رشاد"

Some of the boys had already ripped out their extra socks and wore them while they slept in the cool caves. The cave air thickened with the cold cloud puffs that exited their mouths. The guide told them it was too dangerous to light a fire, so the other four fathers shared their proverbs in the dark.

Yusuf and his sons picked up their prayer mats where they had been placed in a circle and found a warm corner to sleep. After some time passed Yusuf heard the rhythmic sound of both sons' gentle snores. Yusuf's deep slumbering breaths soon joined theirs.

A few hours later movement woke Yusuf, and he turned to see Salih head for the cave entrance. After a moment, Yusuf followed.

Salih had his bag with him. He found a flat rock to sit on and pulled out his mother's mint pouch. Yusuf watched as Salih brought it up to his nose to smell the earthy scent. A tear streaked down Salih's chubby cheek and dragged Yusuf's heart with it. Yusuf wondered if his son was remembering when they first dug up the soil for the mint garden, how Salih had taken his mother's favorite tool and she had to chase him, their laughter echoing off the mountain side.

With soft footsteps, Yusuf's nephew Omar—the second oldest boy in the group—joined him at the cave entrance in watching Salih.

"This journey will change him," Omar whispered. "I know it will change all of us, but Salih is more sensitive and is very attached to his mother."

Yusuf's pulse quickened and he tugged on his beard. "Not having any of you be with your mothers will be a blow to us all. We should be growing old in your homes, not worrying if they will be in our village or in Türkiye."

Yusuf placed his arm around Omar's shoulder as the boy let out a big sigh.

الجبل الأخضر

As Salwa watches them leave, their bodies merging with the rest of the group into one dark form, her body begins to feel heavy. A weight begins to descend on her shoulders, works its way into her heart, and weakens her knees. She wants to give in to the strong pull of the earth to collapse where she stands, but instead she gets to work.

Without the extra pairs of hands, all the chores fall to her. She milks the cow, takes the goat to the upper field, and plucks chicken eggs from their warm nests. While Salwa is turning over a new section in her garden, a group of women and girls from her community join her to help with the labor. The other wives, some who had lost sons to the Colonizers and whose husbands were off fighting in the Capital, are going from farm to farm to help the women who are now alone with their chores and childcare.

Salwa carries the baby in the burlap sling until one of the girls takes her away to play with the others. She only brings her back to feed her. There is no time to play today. There is also not enough time to still the loss that seeps into Salwa's bones.

Even with all the extra help Salwa does not finish all the morning chores until well after the midday sun passes. All the other women left to go help on other farms. She enters the farmhouse—the baby long asleep on her back—and feels the silence. The still air suffocates her. There are no endless questions from Salih followed by the teasing from his older brother. Yusuf's corner is empty, and no sorted piles of seeds adorn the table before his seat. He would only take his eyes off counting them to occasionally tell the boys to quiet down while he tugged his beard, a habit he had when he was deep in thought. Amal would be next to the corner bread stove, pounding flour and reciting prayers to keep away the djinns.

Salwa debates a cup of mint tea but decides to go to Moufida's house for lunch instead. It is her first meal without her family, and she knows that if she doesn't leave soon the silence will choke her completely.

Salwa wishes she could ride her horse, but they sold her to pay the guide, a descendant from the Ottoman soldiers who knew his way through the previously ruled Türkiye cities. He also had the skills to navigate the fierce sandstorms that might otherwise slice through a caravan. Salwa knows the men would not be able to walk the journey alone and need a contact at the orphanage. She still cried for three days when her horse was sold. She did it quietly in her garden, pretending to weed. The horse had been her first gift from her first love, a boy who she watched turn into a man and

then into her husband. He had known her since they were
children and knew how much she loved to ride on the white
beach with the ocean wind blowing in her hair.

So Salwa sets out on foot, carrying a few treasures from
the garden to share. The baby is awake and tied to one hip,
tracing the tattooed lines on her mother's cheek until Salwa
giggles. Although Salwa loves sharing this special moment,
she wishes she had tied the baby onto her back now that she
is getting heavier. They enter the date orchard next to
Moufida's house for a shortcut. The path is well worn from
their boys' heavy use. Salwa stops at the sound of singing
through the trees. She does not know the song for the words
are in the language of the Colonizers.

درنة إلى انطاكية

The thick fog in the valley added a frozen stillness to the
air between the group. It was their nineteenth day of walking.
The green layer of pine needles under their feet kept their
footsteps quiet. The boys' pace slowed, not only from
exhaustion, but also because they were in awe of the
evergreens that surrounded them, similar to the trees in Jabel
Al-Akhdar, but taller.

The guide led them to an abandoned farmhouse nearby
to spend their last day together.

"The orphanage is in the next valley over," the guide
said. "We'll stay here for the rest of the day and night. My
contact there has other Libyan boys and has agreed to protect
as many as needed. His grandfather can tie his family to your
country. Even though the people that run the orphanage do
not speak your language, they pray in the same direction."

The stone house looked like any structure in their village except that parts of the roof were missing. They found a front room to rest in with the least number of holes. The men collected tree branches and wove them to block the sunshine streaming through the opening that once held a door frame. After the room darkened a little the boys rolled out prayer rugs and gathered in two rows with their fathers, standing shoulder to shoulder.

Fethi stood in front of the two rows. The boys had taken turns leading prayers each day of their journey. Fethi had seen his father do this his entire life, but now led his first. Yusuf noticed a shadow growing on his upper lip. He wondered if he would ever see his sons' full beards.

A few of the boys fell asleep during their prayers and the men let them rest—slumped over their prayer maps—while they finished their last salaam.

Once the last boy had fallen asleep, all the men gathered outside to go over the plans for the following day. Yusuf hoped they would all go to the orphanage so he could prepare them for Salih's endless questions. However, they decided it would be better if the guide was the only one who dropped off the boys. After they finalized all the details, they went to sleep.

The next morning, the fathers gathered the sons in a circle after their morning prayers to fill their heads with the last of the proverbs.

Yusuf told the boys around the circle, "He whose covering belongs to others is uncovered."

Everyone went silent as Yusuf went on to explain how it is always better to rely on what is solely owned, as it is safer and more worthy, than to borrow what is not yours. An item lent must always be subject to being recalled by the owner. Once they returned home, Yusuf and his community had full intentions of taking back the land they never agreed to loan.

"المتغطي بمتاع الناس عريان" the boys repeat after Yusuf.

الجبل الأخضر

Salwa crouches but it is too late. She is spotted. She turns to run but he is next to her in no time. The gun sling across his chest bounces as he rushes to grab her arm. His hair is the color of sunshine, and his skin is very pale except for the countless freckles dusting his cheeks. At first, she can't tell where his neck ends and his tan shirt starts. He yanks her arm so hard she yelps.

The baby starts to wail.

"Quiet it down," he hisses to her in his broken Arabic. His formal, bureaucratic, cracking words in her language feel like broken shards of glass in her ears. "Or I do it."

Salwa pats the baby's back with her trembling hand. She keeps her eyes on the soldier as he adjusts the gun sling. Her heartbeat is deafening, and she is sure the birds around her are now quiet because the sound has engulfed them.

"Now set it down so we have fun."

Tears flood Salwa's eyes. There is no point in trying to flee as her body locks up in fear. She has taken this route a million times before, but she is unable to gauge clearly how far back her home is. When she thinks of her farmhouse, she sees Yusuf in her mind. The dread of how she will tell him forces her to her knees.

"I am here to talk to your sheiks about building a road to benefit your people. I had no idea I would also receive a gift." He smirks as he gives her arm another twist. "I said down."

Salwa hunches her shoulders to protect the baby on her hip as she tries to undo the knot of the burlap sling with her rattling hands.

A sudden crack sounds behind her and the full weight of the Colonizer crashes into her. Salwa manages to arch against his body and topple them both to the side to protect the baby. Her child's desperate cries ring out in the orchard; Salwa grasps for her baby and twists to look up. Moufida stands above her, out of breath and holding a bloody rock in her shaking right hand.

"I was already on my way to check on you. I wanted to make sure you were okay. Then I heard the baby and ran." Moufida's voice is choked with anger. She grabs the back of the man's uniform and pulls him off of her neighbor.

They both stand panting over the Colonizer's limp body, and Salwa now fully sees how large he is. There is a bloody gash behind his right ear and blood saturates his near white hair. The earth under his head is starting to turn the same color it does when they sacrifice the Mawlid lamb every year.

"We can't just leave him," Salwa whispers. Her knees give out and she crumbles to the ground again. Her lips tighten and jaw begins to clench at the thoughts that enter her mind of what might have happened had Moufida not arrived at that moment. She wants to scream at the pain from her twisted arm but there is no time to think about it. She haphazardly gathers the baby into her sling and the child buries her face into her mother's wet armpit.

Moufida drops the rock. "You are right. His friends will be here soon looking for him. We have to hide the body."

"We must make it look like an accident." Salwa's breathing begins to even out. The pain in her arm dulls as she pushes it away to the back of her mind.

The baby finally stills but her face is wet with tears. Moufida takes off her head scarf to wipe her down and the baby traces Moufida's facial tattoos with her chubby fingers.

Moufida gives her round cheeks a kiss and tells Salwa, "Grab his ankles. Let's take him to the cliff above the ravine."

Salwa ties the baby to her back, ignores the pain that shoots up her arm as she clutches his boots, and instead gets to work.

انطاكية إلى درنة

Yusuf recognizes many of the landmarks as the men rush back home. Their journey is faster when the boys are not with them, and they make it back to their Jabel Al-Akhdar in half the time. Their guide had bid them farewell before continuing along the coast.

The first smell they notice is death and burning flesh. Then they see the smoke plume rise above their valley. They climb higher on the mountain to hunch down behind a boulder and scout the damage in their village below.

Their livestock is destroyed, their bellows of pain echoing off the juniper trees as most are still on fire. The town well is filled with sand and Yusuf helplessly looks on as his sons' beloved madrasa is run over with a tank. The new Colonizer roads had made it possible for the tanks to navigate deeper into the mountain.

"I'm going to my house to get my gun from the chicken coop," Mustafa declares, and they all follow. "We can look for other survivors, and especially weapons."

Before they reach any of the farms, they are spotted by some Colonizers holding torches and burning the masjid down. Yusuf watches as the red geraniums his wife planted last spring catch on fire, red on red. The five men try to hide, but it is too late.

Yusuf draws his gun and shoots two of the Colonizers before he is shot in the shoulder and stomach.

The world slows as Yusuf falls to his knees. The screams and gunshots grow distant, and he hears his words to his son ring in his ears, "We'll all return home. Inshallah." Smoke wafts from the pile where their home once stood. Yusuf slumps all the way to the ground.

One of the Colonizers limps as he wanders over and crouches before Yusuf. A fresh red scar is above his right ear, and he smirks as Yusuf gasps.

"Well, well, well. Look who is ready to join their wives in the camps."

The Elevator Woman

by
Nayiri Baboudjian Bouchakjian

Déjà vu is perhaps the greatest of phenomena
For none other can be explained
-Malack Jallad

Beirut, May 2006
Apartment 2A

I called the ambulance at 3:15 p.m. Mom's oxygen levels had been dropping gradually, but the doctor asked us to wait until the afternoon. I paced our corridor, praying to all the saints I had grown up with for a miracle: Saint Charbel, Saint Nectarios, Saint Rafka, and Saint Elias. Our next-door neighbor, a devout Catholic hairdresser who had lived in apartment 2B since the 1950s, told me so many stories of miracles that happened to pilgrims who visited Saint Charbel in his Monastery in Annaya, north of Beirut.

My sister placed a pillow under Mom's head to improve her breathing. Mom's oncologist had prepared us for this moment.

"The end will not be peaceful; the end is rarely peaceful, especially with this type of ovarian cancer."

I hated everything about the doctor, from his polo shirt to his matter-of-fact manner of dealing with the end. At times, I had fantasies of him involving plane crashes and mysterious disappearances, perhaps kidnappings. As Mom's breathing grew heavier and the gurgle of fluid crept into her lungs, I prayed for the electricity to stay on until the Red Cross reached our place.

The Red Cross team was one of the most well-organized entities in Beirut. They functioned well under stress. They sure had seen enough crises. The team called my sister at 3:25 p.m. She raced downstairs in three leaps to open the gate.

The metal door squeaked as it gave way to them. By the time they reached the second floor, Mom's cough was more persistent, and she itched her nose as she usually did when she was impatient.

"It's my spring allergy," she wheezed.

We were lucky when our problems were spring allergies. I admired Mom's hair, and the way it had grown in small white curls after stopping her chemotherapy sessions. I even admired the tiny black hairs trying to grow on the side of her lips.

Relief washed over me at the sight of the orange-red costumes and concerned faces of the ambulance team.

"Ya tante, nehna haddik," the team leader said.

The only lady on the team was asking my sister about the elevator as the others transferred Mom to a stretcher.

"We can take the elevator from the third floor, as the lady upstairs has locked it from here," my sister said.

I was my mom's primary caregiver, but my sister had been taking care of all outside matters—hospital bed, oximeter, oxygen machine, morphine patches. The team leader explained to my sister that having access to the elevator would help, as Mom's condition was delicate, but after explaining matters to the team, they decided to go up to the third floor and then take the elevator down to the ground floor. Knowing that the elevator was locked from the first floor also, the team members debated the pros and cons of climbing up one floor versus going down two floors.

As our procession headed to the third floor, other neighbors opened their doors and expressed their concern, waved at us, and crossed their faces. My sister pressed on the button of the third-floor elevator. I prayed again that the electricity would stay with us for five more minutes.

Mom was almost in the elevator when Madame Yvette, with her slim chignon, opened her door across the hall and blurted out, "Vous ne pouvez pas utiliser cet ascenseur."

The EMTs, unfamiliar with a very familiar dispute in the building, looked surprised but continued their work. It was only when she went up a notch and almost screamed, claiming ownership of the elevator, that the team leader spoke to her in curt sentences.

"Madame, do you know who we are? What if she was your own sister or daughter?"

The insults continued. Madame Yvette cursed the Red Cross team for using the elevator that she had unashamedly locked from the second and first floors. It was a privilege that she had inherited from her father-in-law, who had built the building in the 1940s. He had carefully made arrangements with the builders to install the elevator—thinking that the lives of the sick and old tenants would be easier.

"Non, non, merde. Non, non!!"

Her daughter, who had been shadowing her, tried to pull her inside, complaining that she had embarrassed her yet another time. I caught a glimpse of her daughter's hands. The skin was angry red and severely inflamed. Again.

When Mom and I were in the safety of the ambulance, I nearly collapsed. I reminded myself that the timing of the electricity was perfect, at least. I held Mom's hand through a series of bumps and dips in the road. There was no radio, so the EMTs hushed conversation carried to the back.

I could hear the team leader whisper to himself, "Hayaweneh hal marah, shou hayaweneh. May God forgive her."

I was not going to cry in front of people. I had actually developed a technique back in the days of the Civil War. When my tears knocked uninvited, I would pinch my hand lightly. I would then increase the pressure slowly.

The ambulance ride seemed long. Ambulances are never fast enough. I could feel my heart beat so fast, as if I needed to run to keep up with it. I couldn't help but remember the endless Saturday mornings when Madame Yvette would come to our house for coffee. She made it a point to bring the coffee with her. And her chignon. I thought my mom and Yvette were friends. So did my mom. I wondered if Mom also grieved fading friendships.

During the Civil War, the elevator woman was still bearable in ways that allowed her to have coffee with her neighbors every Saturday. But then, sometime in the early 2000s, she cut the cord that tied her to her neighbors and became reclusive. She went out rarely, and only if one of the neighbors passed away. During those occasions of mourning, she was usually the first one there paying her respects, and she made sure to stay for hours. She would carry her perfectly coiffed and heavily sprayed chignon like a duty as she cried for her neighbors and told stories of World War II in France.

"We had to wait in line for bread...."

For her neighbors, it was déjà vu.

"You should not throw away bread. Mais non.... Bake it in the oven, and voila, use it in Fattouch. Just don't throw away bread."

For years to come, and generations to follow, Madame Yvette's family members would feel the burden of her animosity—they would shamefully apologize on her behalf and avoid the topic of the elevator at all costs. They would have to deal with the guilt, just like they had to deal with their sister's OCD—the obsessive handwashing that peeled away her skin, that delayered it like a helpless onion.

***

Beirut, June 2013
Apartment 3B

They told me later on that it was his first time in the Mouradian Building. Someone must have seen him downstairs and assisted him to the third floor. He could not see much. Madame Zahraa—who had come to visit her daughter in the building facing ours—told us that he was completely blind and walked with a stick, but Abou Tony—the owner of the grocery store—swore that the gentleman who walked into the Mouradian Building on that beautiful June morning could partially see. Shades. Colors. Both Madame Zahraa and Abou Tony agreed that the gentleman

108

entered about the time when everyone in our building had woken up and was sipping coffee slowly. Our building itself goes into coffee break modes during lazy mid-morning chats. The real owner of our building, may God have mercy on his soul, chose the best building materials. He told my husband that many times. The location that he chose, also, is gold. Enveloped between two parallel roads, our building is sandwiched between jasmine bushes on the left and a multi-rooted frangipani tree on the right. And June is the month of beautiful scents.

I must have been on the balcony when I heard some noise from the apartment next door. I had just finished hanging the laundry outside on the balcony facing the Armenian Evangelical Church. It's not that easy to put the laundry out. One has to be careful with what one reveals, and of course, one has to respect order. The lingerie, men's underwear, and all the intimate items of clothing have to be on the inner lining—no one is meant to see our intimate clothing—just like no one is meant to know of the conversations that happen within our homes. The trousers, tops, and skirts can be on the middle clothesline, but always hidden by the bed sheets and tablecloths.

I was used to commotion from Madame Yvette's apartment. A deceivingly quiet woman, she screamed at anyone who attempted to use the elevator. I avoided her as much as I could and detested her attitude. On that specific day, I knew from the rhythmic slapping of her Aleppo ghapghaps that she was up to trouble as she approached to open the door. My husband had asked me not to intervene in Yvette's ordeals, so I resorted to the peephole to make sure things did not get out of control. I told all the other neighbors

109

what happened on that specific day, as that gentleman from the Organization of the Blind mistakenly knocked on Yvette's door. Of course, it took me a long time to piece all the events together. We used to also order rose water and orange blossom from the same organization, but we stopped a long time ago. I used to drink orange blossom mixed with water and a spoonful of sugar. They helped with my panic attacks. That was when my mother-in-law lived with us. God rest her soul.

On that day, I imagined Yvette as a little devilish woman, hurrying to open her door, ready for her element, spilling out insults.

"Aman, aman, who? No! Don't tell me you used the elevator!"

The anger in her voice almost hid the fragility of a woman in her eighties. My husband insists that women calm down after sixty.

Yvette's insults are déjà vu for me and the other neighbors. But for the gentleman from the Organization, they must have been new.

"Hello Mrs. Noran, I'm Tony, from the Organization of the Blind. You had ordered rose wa—"

The sword of her voice cut his ambitions into a million pieces.

"Aman, aman, these people will not learn. What rose water? I ordered nothing! And you probably used the elevator! May God take you to Jehannam—because this is where you belong. Crazy boy! How dare you use this elevator? You know this building belongs to us. Only us! Now off you go to Jehannam, and make sure you take the stairs."

I could guess the contours of his face as he tried to open his mouth and speak, but words jammed in his throat.

"I said off you go! Can't you hear me? Or are you deaf also? Didn't you read the paper downstairs that says not to use this elevator?"

I spotted Madame Mary from the fourth floor walking down the stairs, struggling with her cane, but of course avoiding the elevator. I was tempted to open the door. One should not miss out on such fights. They do not happen every day. Akh, akh. My husband is so stingy when it comes to us participating in such ordeals, even refusing to install a new peephole. I have to enjoy them from the privacy of our home.

The voices of some other neighbors outside interjected as they tried to interfere in the most recent dispute on the Mouradian Building's elevator. It reminded me of the time, years ago, when Yvette had stopped the Red Cross members from helping Madame Ani, our second-floor neighbor. God rest her soul.

And now, tell me, why should I feel guilty for not opening our door?

***

Beirut, August 20, 2020
Apartment 2A

There is something hostile about the humidity of Beirut in August. Sometime in July, it becomes almost impossible to live without an AC. With the more frequent electricity cuts, my husband and I each have a fan. Yes, ones like Oscar Wilde probably used when he wrote *Lady Windermere's Fan*.

We sit in our salon overlooking the Port of Beirut and laugh at ourselves using dainty fans. Mine is a red one that I hold close to my heart. It is a souvenir that my boss Surayya gave me after her vacation in Spain. My husband's is the lacy white one I used on our wedding day. We need reasons to laugh. Life has become a matter of priority and selection.

"I am OK with no electricity, but I cannot do without water."

Deprived of electricity and water, we have created other ways of bypassing the heat. We wash our faces with ice cubes and sometimes let the ice particles drop down our shoulders. We buy bottled Tannourine water and sprinkle it over each other. Intimacy has not been on our minds, but every now and then, we hug each other. We are careful not to hug too hard; we respect the bruises.

There is something about summers in Beirut. Add dynasties of flies to the humidity. Flies are everywhere, and my fear is that they will get inside my ear. Who would have thought that even the powerful Mouradian Building would shed its glasses in just seconds, and we would have to dress it up with nylon? After the Port of Beirut explosions there were no windows or doors left. So much glass shattered. So much of the glass from our windows ended up on the streets, in books, in underwear drawers. Until, of course, some NGO comes by and considers renovating our windows. And our doors. And the façade of the building. With these temporary nylon replacements, the heat has doubled.

Almost fifteen days after the blast we still find glass in the house. Glass in the cupboards, glass in our closets, glass in our clothes. Of course, we are the lucky ones because glass did not find our eyes. Because we only have a few bruises of mauve and blue. I never thought that my skin could turn so blue overnight. Of course, we are the lucky ones because we are still breathing in the heat and humidity of Beirut.

The bright red abat-jours so typical of the buildings in this part of town will disappear somehow. Different NGOs will take over the renovation of different floors. The Mouradian Building, which has endured a fifteen-year-old Civil War, the 2006 Israeli invasion, many assassinations, street fights, and family disputes, will finally give in to the Port of Beirut blast aftershocks. The first-floor balcony window will eventually turn grey with iron bars, resembling a prison cell.

It's not safe around here anymore, Madame Randa will explain. The third floor will turn darker red—the NGO will eventually convince the ailing Yvette that darker colors are more fit for her abat-jours. It's also about availability, they will explain. The fourth-floor balcony will stay naked and colorless for a while. The fifth floor is now an Airbnb apartment. It's hard to believe that there are no constant neighbors on the fifth floor.

The Norwegian NGO that will take care of the façade of the five buildings near the Armenian Evangelical Church will erase the marks of the Civil War. They have already told us that at this point food is the priority, but they will help us cover the two huge dents on the side of the fifth floor.

"Your building looks tired," the NGO representative says. "We will make it look younger. We will cover all the holes. All the imperfections."

I remember when I was eight, Madame Yvette's daughter got injured while she was on the balcony. It was the shrapnel. She must have been hanging the washing—all in meticulous order. It was difficult to find a hospital then. But she survived. Except for her hands.

We did not care about the dents and the holes the bombs left on the side of the third-floor balcony.

For days after the explosion, we did not have electricity or internet. Friends and family members would frantically call our landline, hear our voices, cry, and hang up. They would call again. Windows can be fixed, they would say. Foreign news says that the Port explosion was the third largest explosion of all time. Was that a privilege to internalize? What do we do with that? Do we add it to our CV and boast that we have survived the third largest explosion?

I have not left the house since the explosion. My husband goes out every morning to buy bread and other necessities. We have not been cooking much. There is no time to cook. I wash the floors every day, and every day, I find that soot and black ash particles return. I don't need to use Clorox. We are forced to put COVID on hold. My husband tells me to be careful with glass, that 56 people have lost their eyesight. All of these 56 residents live in Jemmayze—a five-minute walk from our house. Our first-floor neighbor, an elderly gentleman in his eighties already suffering with end-stage Alzheimer's, was completely thrown off his bed from the power of the blast. He is still alive. His wife says she wishes he had died.

We have not been sitting on our balcony, which used to be a source of pride for overlooking the Mediterranean.

These are times when we thank God for the dead. I thank God that my dad passed away in January, seven months before the explosions. He would have died an uglier death had he still been alive. Uglier than Alzheimer's. The balcony door was uprooted from its hinges and landed on Dad's bed. Dad's bed was empty then. I thanked God for the timing.

There is a question that I have been meaning to ask my husband, but cannot bring myself to. Every day after he comes back home, after his daily round in the neighborhood, he gives me updates about neighbors. And every day, I avoid asking him the question.

As we sip our coffee quietly this sweltering August day, he tells me nonchalantly, "She is still alive, you know? She made it."

He has read my mind.

He goes on, "She needs to have two or three surgeries—broken shoulder, hand…."

I feel relieved.

Immediately after the explosions on August 4, when all doors were gaping open and a collective malaise of screams, cries, loss, and helplessness hung in the air, we heard third-floor neighbors screaming for help. Other neighbors called the Red Cross, but it was almost impossible for the team to reach to our building. They tried. But roads were full of glass and debris, and also people…injured, dying, and in between.

I heard the elevator woman's cries as she struggled to walk down the stairs. Her son was holding her by the right hand, and her brother-in-law by the left one. Still in her combinaison, they practically dragged her down the stairs. Blood covered her face and arms. No one had bothered to cover her shoulders. It was the first time I saw the elevator lady use the stairs in so many years. When she had heard the initial airplane at around 6:06 p.m., she had rushed to the balcony to see what the smoke was all about. After the explosions had ripped Beirut apart, she had found herself on the floor in the living room.

At times, the timing of electricity was just imperfect.

***

Beirut, July 20, 2022
Apartments 1A, 1B, 2A, 2B, 3A, 3B, 4A, 4B, 5A, 5B

We go to the supermarket today. We buy cheese. We skip the labne. We buy bread. We skip the jambon and turkey. At times, we even skip the toilet paper. We don't need to tell friends about this. We use tissue paper—the cheapest kind. It feels so rough.

We crave cherries and give in to the temptation. We buy one kilo of cherries from the grocery store up the road. There are different types, he says, at 35,000 LL, 45,000 LL, and 55,000 LL. The ones that are being sold at 55,000 LL smile at us. We don't tell our neighbors that we are buying the most affordable ones. Some things should not be shared with even the closest neighbors.

We wait in line for bread—some people manage to buy two rabta-s of Lebanese bread. When our turn comes, the manager at the bakery tells us that there is only brown bread. "No more white," mechanically uttered. We buy brown bread.

We buy flour.

We wait until our sister, mother, father, brother, son, daughter, cousin, relative, sends us fresh dollars from abroad. Then we rush to the exchange, but hesitate. Should we do this today or tomorrow? The rate today is 29,000 Lebanese Liras for every dollar. Tomorrow, it may shoot up to 32,000 LL. Remember? This is what happened two months ago.

Once we exchange the $100, we rush back home with a short-lived euphoria. On the entrance of the building, we see the man who collects money for the generator subscription.

"It's 3.5 million this month," he says, keeping the poker face. "For five amps."

The 2,900,000 LL that we just exchanged. Right on time. But not enough. Another hundred.

And another.

We need to buy water. We haven't had water for five days now. It's almost 800,000 LL for 2,000 liters. The water is not clean, but we need water. Any water.

We want to fill up our cars with fuel. We want to fill up our phones with credit. We want to be connected. We need internet. We need to move around. We need medications. We ask friends to send us Panadol. Advil. Insulin. Blood pressure medications. Friends of friends.

We go to the supermarket and buy a few items. We buy labne. We skip the cheese. We buy thyme. We skip the olive oil. We mix the labne with the thyme. We crave to buy Vileda sponges. Skip. We crave hotdogs. Skip. Three cheese. Four cheese. Our favorite type of cornflakes sits on the shelf. We greet the box in silence. We buy Nescafe.

We come back home. It's hot and humid. We are tired. Our legs hurt. We carry the bags with us to the building. We head to the elevator. Our partner jokes at us for heading to the elevator. We must have forgotten for that one second that the elevator is now just another box in the building. Built by the Austrian Sowitsch Aufzug Company in 1952, the elevator wallows in its aloneness.

We struggle with our ailing knees and painful backs. We take the stairs slowly. Greet the neighbors on each floor. The bags are not heavy at all.

We are, after all, the poorest millionaires.

At times, the timing of the electricity is non-existent.

At times, even the elevator smells of corruption.

Welcome Home

by
Alizeh Farhad

Like the seas of salt and sweet
that meet but do not mix
There exist
borders
lines
signs
If only they knew that their attempt to divide would be met
with bitterness

-Malack Jallad

Unaccompanied Women and Minors

Roxy focuses on the familiar grey signboard, its fading off-white letters unapologetically commanding the attention of all eyes entering the lobby. She scans the room, pausing only momentarily at its counterpart, an identical grey plate stating *All Arriving Passengers*.

The endless queue at the immigration counter is exclusively men, several with either sleeping infants adorning their shoulders or energized children running noisily between the line and the benches in the sitting area where the women are waiting.

119

She half nods and mutters, "Rush hour at the airport indeed."

Roxy glances back at the unaccompanied women's line, where an elderly woman in a wheelchair is being assisted by airport staff. The only other passenger in that line is a frazzled mother traveling with her three young children, who are prancing in circles around her.

It would be wise to wait a few minutes before getting in line behind the young mother…and maybe even better to wait until they're done.

Yes, she would wait. Her gaze shifts back to the sign.

Unaccompanied Women

It is equal parts incredible and amusing that despite over a decade of traveling through this airport, the signage and its underlying principles irk Roxy with renewed fervor. To be likened to a vulnerable child, simply because she is a woman traveling without the "protection" of a man—that's just plain ridiculous!

Then there's the issue of the separate queue, as if an unaccompanied woman deserves preferential treatment due to her uninformed mind. And she's simultaneously a dangerous entity—one that shouldn't be allowed to mingle with the rest, the *All Arriving Passengers* lest she somehow corrupt them with her nonconformist thoughts and actions.

She lets out a sigh. It would not serve her well to go down this spiral, especially not right now. She looks past the terminal exit and reflects on the fact that her father, the only male in her family, would not be waiting outside to pick her up and bring her home. This time, she would have to navigate the city on her own and address his myriad estate matters, ironically as an unaccompanied woman.

But as much as the sign at the airport questions her personhood and competence, she knows she's ready to bend or break any rules to accomplish her goal.

She opens her backpack, grabs the large pashmina shawl she packed in there, and drapes it around herself. She takes extra care to stretch the shawl to cover her V-neck, her short sleeves, and, most importantly, the top of her jeans and the curve of her behind. Once she's satisfied with the outcome, she glances back at the line.

The young family is collecting their documents from the immigration officer, so she grabs her carry-on bag and proceeds to the desk.

The officer's gaze is fixed on a document as she approaches, but he nonetheless extends his hand for her passport. Roxy hands it over. It's a local passport, so the booklet echoes the same shade of deep green as the flag on the officer's desk, and he misses not a beat in turning to the biometric data page. He knows this passport, reads right to left, and does not seek the explanations she has become accustomed to providing to the English-speaking universe.

"Miss Rakhshanda," he says, glancing up.

Roxy instinctively looks straight into his eyes, momentarily mesmerized by the beauty of this perfect rendition of her given name—the low growl of the "R" and the husky grunt of the "kh" both correctly emphasized.

A split second later, she realizes her mistake. She's Miss Rakhshanda now, and respectable, cultured women named Miss Rakhshanda do not defiantly meet men's gazes. It's as if the operating system in her brain has suddenly been booted into *Safe Mode*, with the updates and security patches acquired through life's experiences disabled and only the basic features left intact.

She lowers hers gaze and responds, in the softest tone she can muster, "Jee sir."

"Which flight have you come on?" he asks.

"Dubai se Sir. Flight number boarding pass par likha hua hai."

Roxy takes extra precaution to ensure that she inserts these Urdu words and that her diction affirms the suggestion her passport has made—that she is one of them, a local, not a snooty expat. A little green stamp on her customs declaration would easily save her an hour, and appealing to this officer's sense of compatriotism is critically needed to earn that.

With the first battle won, Roxy marches over to the luggage carousel. It's now only a matter of minutes before she can exit the terminal building. She recognizes her suitcase at the far end of the carousel gliding smoothly towards her. She reaches toward her suitcase but is intercepted by a man in a khaki uniform who climbs atop the conveyer belt and lifts up her bag with both his arms.

"Madam, you will need a porter," he says with commanding confidence.

Roxy grabs the handle. "No, I do not need a porter. I can carry my bags myself." She tries to hide the exasperation in her voice. She tugs at it until he releases his hold.

And so it begins, she thinks to herself. These small, seemingly harmless violations of her independence. She reminds herself it is only for three weeks, and concludes, as she has every time, that for all she stands to gain, this is a price she is willing to pay.

***

Outside the airport terminal, Farzana waits for her niece's arrival. It's been eight years since her sister's family visited the homeland. They fled in a rush after Ahmed bhai's sudden death, and the lingering effects of that trauma had kept them away.

"But why did they decide to send Rakhshanda? She's barely lived here as an adult. What does she even know of how this place works?"

She realizes she has voiced her thoughts out loud when she finds her husband shooting her an inquiring look. She merely shakes her head in response.

"The flight from Dubai arrived almost 45 minutes ago. She should come out any minute now," she says.

Farzana's statement is met with a disinterested grunt from her husband—he is not particularly enthusiastic about being dragged to the airport at 1 a.m. to pick up her niece. He doesn't ever miss a chance to indicate his dislike of her family. According to him, they don't give him the respect a man deserves. And he considers it the epitome of that disrespect that they've insisted Farzana's inheritance assets be kept exclusively in her name.

Oh well. Farzana continues her dialogue internally. It's usually more prolific than conversing with her husband anyway.

She notices a solitary tall female form in the distance. Although her face is unrecognizable yet, Farzana is convinced it is Rakhshanda. This is not your usual local woman. Instead, she exudes a confidence and energy that makes you think she owns the earth you're standing on.

Farzana turns to her husband with the smile of a child in a candy store. "She's here."

***

As Roxy steps from the air-conditioned building into the warm, humid night, she reminisces about the unfailing bliss this moment has always evoked. The hot, sticky air engulfing her feels like wet kisses in a mother's embrace. The scent in the air is sea and earth, mixed in with a little bit of displaced desert. This moment of homecoming is special for her—it's as if she's crossed the proverbial Platform 9 ¾ into a world where she belongs. Like a piece of a jigsaw puzzle that has, at long last, finally landed in its right place.

Roxy spots Farzana Khala—Fuzzy Khala as they've always called her. The gray hair flecking Fuzzy Khala's temples and the stoop in her posture give Roxy a momentary jolt. Clearly, time hasn't shied from collecting its dues. But that's to be expected—most of all from the place that violently robbed her of her father.

Anger rises within her at that thought. She gives herself a minute to let the emotion pass, but she's not so lucky. The stabbing feeling in her chest is soon accompanied by stinging in her eyes. Her family has spent nearly a decade running away from this confrontation. It is silly of her to think it would pass so soon. But there is a reason why she's the one who had to come back—she's the most cool-headed, the only one who can overcome this emotionality and move on to business.

Taking a deep breath, she approaches her family and calls out.

"Fuzzy Khala! I'm finally here!"

124

***

The drive from the airport to Roxy's house is long, crossing nearly the entire city. Roxy is quiet, staring out the rolled-down window and taking in the sights. She knows she shouldn't talk. Her uncle is visibly in a bad mood. But then again, Roxy cannot recall a time in their acquaintance when he hasn't been in a foul mood.

It is nearly 2 a.m. but the city seems bright and awake. Streetside food stalls serve young men who sit at tables on the sidewalks under the streetlights. Old Bollywood music blares loudly from portable radios set up in the stalls. There are Carrom boards at one end of the sidewalk, and groups of young boys appear to be engaged in spirited Carrom competitions. The carefree laughter of youth fills the air.

The car stops at a red light and a young boy rushes up to them, jasmine bud garlands in hand. He implores them to buy the last of his batch. Deeply inhaling her favorite fragrance, Roxy remembers the countless times her mom asked her dad to oblige similar requests. Roxy smiles and turns her head toward her uncle, aiming to do the same. The vexed expression on his face, however, stops the words from leaving her mouth. She looks away.

They go over the bridge that connects the old and new cities—a bridge Roxy used to cross every day as a teenager when her father taught her how to drive. She chuckles as she recalls how she would inevitably stall the stick shift vehicle at the top of the bridge due to nervousness, and her dad would preemptively pull the emergency brake. Her high school classmates regularly witnessed this event and never let her live it down. As a consequence of this, she insists on

125

driving a car with a manual transmission, and prides herself on stall-free starts on hills of any steepness.

The old neighborhood slowly approaches. Roxy's stomach churns. The thumping of her heart becomes deafening. And then she sees it. The street corner with the ATM—the place where an unnecessary struggle between an armed robber and a naïve civilian resulted in two shots being fired. One took down the poor soul trying to save his few rupees, and the other hit a bystander—Roxy's father.

The street is alive with activity. There's a faint sound of music coming from the tea stall—old classics from the '60s playing on the radio. Men sitting on a traditional wooden dais are engaged in a game of cards. Roxy looks at the group reproachfully. Clearly the area is not safe. Why would they be so reckless to loiter about at two in the morning?

Her derisive snort startles Farzana, who turns around just in time to see Roxy rolling her eyes.

"This is just how we live," Farzana says. "In spite of dangers, the force of life persists."

Farzana's emphatic words fall on deaf ears, because Roxy's mind has already surrendered to the blazing fires of anger.

***

Chirppppp. The sound of birds...heralding the arrival of a bright new day.

Something doesn't sound quite right about these birds though.

These persistently squealy birds.

Angry Birds.

126

Roxy nearly loses her balance as she jumps out of bed, realization having struck her that the angry birds are meant to beckon her to the door. She glances at her bedraggled self in the mirror, pats her head in an attempt to tame her hair, and grabs the shawl slung over the dining room chair, draping it over her shoulders as she beelines to the apartment entrance.

The doorbell chirps again, echoing through the apartment as she turns the bolt and reaches for the door handle. The early morning visitor is a young woman who appears to be about the same age as her. She has an oval face with large, kind brown eyes and a soft smile that puts Roxy slightly at ease regarding her unexpected guest.

"Assalam Alaikum. I am Sahr….Mrs. Sahr Ehtesham from apartment 5C. My husband found out from the doorman this morning you had come in late last night, and I thought you might like some hot breakfast."

Roxy looks at Sahr. She is carrying a cream-colored melamine tray bearing a tumbler with hot chai and a plate with fresh potato-stuffed parathas. The added visual makes the tension in her muscles relax and she smiles back, albeit cautiously.

"Wa Alaikum Assalam. I am Rakhshanda."

The name feels as alien as the greeting…distant remnants of a past she makes an effort not to dwell on.

Nevertheless, she finds herself exclaiming, "Thank you so much! It is so very kind of you, but you really shouldn't have. They look positively delicious though."

She takes the tray from Sahr and apologizes for not inviting her in since her apartment is not in any condition to entertain yet. Sahr nods and offers to send her house help to

Roxy later in the day in case Roxy is looking for routine domestic staff.

"Yes! That would be most helpful. The apartment has been locked up for the past eight years, so I will definitely need all the hands I can find to get it back into an inhabitable state. Thank you."

"Of course! And we are right here. I am home all day, so anything you need...just come ring my bell. I will bring you some bottled water too, until you have a filter set up."

Sahr looks straight up at Roxy as she speaks and continues on with a smile.

"My brother is in the same shoes as you—he has been living in Germany for the last 15 years, so I can appreciate what it's like to return home to a dusty apartment and an empty kitchen during these visits. Once you are all settled in, come over for lunch some day and we can chat! You must still be jetlagged, so I'll leave you to it for now."

Roxy can hear her belly growling as she turns away from the door. The tray of parathas and chai looks irresistible. It's her favorite breakfast combo, and to have scored it within hours of landing here can only be a harbinger of good things to come during this trip.

She chuckles at her silly superstitious thought and shifts her thoughts to Sahr. She likes Sahr's open and kind demeanor. It is only a first impression, but a good one at least.

Roxy is not surprised by her neighbor's thoughtfulness and generosity. It is a cultural norm—or it certainly was during her childhood. She can't help but revel in the fact that some good things have remained unchanged. As a child, she spent nearly half her days at her neighbor Mrs. Beg's house.

Mrs. Beg—Batool aunty as she had been to Roxy then. Her mouth curves again, this time into a frown. She feels the muscles in her neck stiffen back up. Mrs. Beg had made many good impressions. Too bad they were not lasting.

Batool aunty had moved into apartment 5B when Rakhshanda was in kindergarten. Her son Ali was the same age as Rakhshanda and enrolled in the same school. As expected, it was only a matter of time before Rakhshanda and Ali became playmates, best friends, and confidants. Every day at 4 p.m., Rakhshanda would go over to Ali's place, sit at his dining table, and work on school assignments with him. At 6 p.m., Batool aunty would furnish them with glasses of fresh carrot juice and Ali would wince—he hated carrot juice. He would begrudgingly drink it nonetheless, because it seemed futile to complain to his mother when his partner-in-crime would be gulping it down greedily.

On weekends they would play for hours with her Lego sets and Ali's car collections. They would read mystery novels and make grand plans about becoming professional detectives. In the evenings, they would go to the apartment complex yard and play cricket or badminton with other neighborhood kids. Rakhshanda and Ali were inseparable, and for this dynamic duo the world was their oyster.

It was in fifth grade when Rakhshanda first noticed the oyster shell cinching in around her. It was an afternoon when she and Ali were working on a math project and realized they needed a few supplies. The stationery store was right down the street, so Ali notified his mother they were going to head down there to pick up some things.

"You can go, but Rakhshanda is not appropriately dressed to go there with you."

Batool aunty's sudden proclamation did not make any sense to Rakhshanda. She was wearing an outfit her mom had given her for her eleventh birthday three months ago— a knee-length pink skirt and a printed T-shirt with pink flowers on it. It was her most favorite thing in the world!

Batool aunty went on. "Rakhshanda—you need to start being careful about these things now. Young women should dress modestly when they leave their houses."

Ali looked back at Rakhshanda's face with equal bewilderment but thought better than to ask his mother to elaborate. The tone of his mother's voice had that stern edge that indicated this was not a matter for discussion. So he just shrugged and picked up the samples for the stationery store, leaving Rakshanda at the table—alone.

That was the last time Rakhshanda wore a skirt outside her house.

A couple of weeks later when Rakhshanda stopped by to ask Ali to play badminton with her, Batool aunty handed her a shawl.

"Cover yourself up with this if you are going to dally about in the yard, though these are really not the types of things for a girl to do." Her face was serious, her knitted brow demonstrating the intensity of her disapproval.

Batool aunty continued to offer instructive advice to Rakhshanda every chance she got thereafter. She did not feel comfortable bringing Rakshanda with her family to an amusement park anymore. She simply did not want to be responsible for someone else's daughter in a public place. She did not think martial arts was a useful or appropriate activity for girls. She would speak to other aunties in the apartment complex about keeping their daughters sheltered and safe like gold jewelry. She would stop by Rakshanda's house and encourage her parents to consider moving her to an all-girls school, where she would learn home economics and cooking instead of sports and karate.

By the end of that school year Rakhshanda's life had changed. She rarely went to Batool aunty's house anymore—she just didn't feel welcome there. While Ali formed a neighborhood cricket league, Rakhshanda began to spend her hours reading. Her parents found it amusing that she had begun to take an interest in crocheting over Legos, but chalked it up to adolescence. They did relocate her to an all-girls Catholic school due to the superior academic performance of their students in national exams, but remained wholly unaware of the impact the neighborly interactions had had on their impressionable child. Rakshanda seemingly thrived and fully applied herself in her new school. She excelled academically and made new friends, so there was no reason for anyone to believe her choices were not merely the outcome of her own changing preferences.

The Begs still lived next door when Rakshanda left the country for college. She had all of her teen years to watch Ali's life unfold—from his under-nineteen cricket nomination to his national debate competition travels. The footprint of his life expanded, and all the while she stayed home. She read and talked on the phone with friends because it was not even permissible for girls to congregate in public places in the evenings. She really liked her Catholic school, and she loved the bond she shared with her friends. But it was hard to not contrast Ali's proverbial oyster against the backdrop of her own life—a life that kept clamming up.

Her parents were ecstatic when she aced the national exams and got a scholarship to study abroad. They threw a grand farewell party, inviting over all the neighbors. That was the last time she saw Mrs. Beg.

Her final words of advice still burned in Roxy's mind.

"Your parents are doing you a disservice. Women need protection. Stop yourself from this terrible mistake while you still have time."

Rakhshanda did not feel upset about Mrs. Beg's commentary. She might vehemently disagree with Mrs. Beg's perspective, but she also knew that the intent behind this suggested bubble-wrapping of her life was to protect her. Her empathy, however, did nothing to make the endeavor feel less suffocating.

A loud grumbling complaint from her belly brings Roxy back into the room with the delectable parathas. Apparently her memories had gotten the best of her.

She breaks off a piece of the flatbread and puts it into her mouth after dousing it in the green chutney that accompanies the bread. The crispiness of the paratha, the creaminess of the spiced potato stuffing, and the burst of herby freshness from the chutney is a symphony in every bite. Sahr certainly knows how to get someone's day off to a good start. She wonders what Sahr thinks of the fact that Roxy is living in her apartment alone. Would she empathize with Roxy, or would she also, like Mrs. Beg, draw up a list of scandalous inadequacies in Roxy's life choices? Well, three weeks was plenty of time to find out.

Until then, there were parathas.

***

Two days later Roxy considers herself reasonably settled in. The apartment has been deep-cleaned and the kitchen has been stocked. Sahr has been true to her word and helped Roxy whenever she's asked. Their encounters have been very enjoyable, and Roxy has seen no reason to amend her first impression. She's even planning to have lunch with Sahr today.

Roxy is also pretty pleased with how streamlined the process to get documents from the national records registry has been. She has dreaded going there for months, expecting it to be the worst bureaucratic nightmare of her lifetime. To think that walking into the registry and scanning the bar code on her national ID card followed by biometric validation got her the requested documents within 60 minutes—documents that her mom has been asking her uncles to assist with obtaining for the last eight years—is flabbergasting. And she would love to be flabbergasted in this manner much more frequently.

Roxy walks down the short hallway to apartment 5C. She hopes her white cotton T-shirt and capris will keep her cool in the afternoon heat. She has chosen to gift a box of dark chocolate truffles she had picked up from her town's local chocolatier to Sahr and hopes that her hostess has a sweet tooth to match hers.

Sahr's house help receives Roxy and directs her to the living room. A few minutes later, Sahr emerges from the bedroom, dressed casually in an oversized T-shirt and cropped tights. Her hair is pulled back into a high ponytail and the softness of her eyes is magnified by her dark rimmed glasses. This is the first time Roxy has seen Sahr wear anything other than a traditional outfit, and she thinks it makes Sahr look barely older than a high school student.

"I am so sorry I didn't meet you at the door. I was trying to finish my notes on this chapter. My Master's thesis is due in six weeks, and I am trying to get ahead of the deadline. By the way, love those capris!"

Roxy is surprised by Sahr's revelation. "Oh, you're in graduate school?"

"Yeah. I worked as a banking executive prior to getting married. But I've wanted to study history—the Bronze Age specifically—ever since my ninth-grade field trip to Mohenjo-daro. Ehtesham thinks he would like a wife who stays at home, so I'm indulging him for now. But once my thesis is approved, I have every intention to look for teaching positions. I have zero aspirations for the life of a permanent housewife."

Roxy is struck by Sahr's unpretentious honesty. On the one hand, Sahr unabashedly accepts that she is fanning her husband's chauvinistic ego, while on the other, she explicitly asserts her independence and ambition.

The lunch hour passes quickly as Roxy and Sahr bond over their experiences in navigating a nonlinear, confounding world. Sahr's insights are profound and witty. Roxy does not find them to be edged with bitterness like hers, and she wonders how Sahr has evaded this cynicism.

Roxy decides to broach the topic. "Does it not bother you when people draw parallels between your entire existence and an object, like a piece of gold to be kept under lock and key?"

Sahr laughs loudly. "Hardly. Condescension is so blind it is amusing."

Roxy looks at her quizzically, imploring her to continue.

"I don't want to suggest we don't have a problem. We really do, but I will also admit that I have no qualms about leveraging the problem where I can for my benefit. I treat life as I would a strategy game. There are some battles you concede, because they give you an overall advantage in the war."

Sahr's fierce words don't match Roxy's initial perception of her as a mellow housewife at all.

"As to your original analogy of being compared to gold—don't you think it's rather apt in a twisted way? Gold might be precious, and you may think it is something that needs your protection. But gold isn't fragile. It doesn't corrode, rust, or tarnish. It can freaking withstand fire. The thought that it needs you to defend it is merely your own delusion. And doesn't it sound just silly?"

Roxy isn't sure yet whether she agrees with Sahr's perspective. But it's definitely food for thought. Sahr is wiser than what Roxy had originally given her credit for. And this is a revised impression she is very happy to have.

**

It is close to the end of the first week of her trip, and Roxy is waiting at the lawyer's office. Lining up the government permits has been easier than she expected, and for this she is glad. Because the excruciating challenges of mundane things like opening a bank account without a male benefactor have stupefied her. Today has been a particularly bad day, and she feels close to the brink of an emotional explosion.

She wants to submit a request for letters of administration to the probate court. This is the final step in the process for transfer of property ownership. She has heard the right lawyer can get it approved in fourteen days. She does not know how to find said right lawyer, so she has chosen instead to go with one of Google's top recommendations for a family lawyer. There is at least a sliver of hope that she will be able to wrap things up during this trip.

At the annoying but persistent urging of her mother, Roxy has brought her eighteen-year-old cousin Irfan along with her. Her mother's words continue to echo in her ears.

"Women don't belong in these offices. But since you won't listen to reason, you have to at least let Irfan accompany you."

And so, Irfan is now sitting across from her in the waiting room, engrossed in his cell phone.

The lawyer, an older gentleman, walks through the waiting room into his office. He is the same generation as her mother. Roxy suspects this meeting will keep with the theme of the day she's had so far. She hopes she is just being overly cynical because of her cranky mood.

The lawyer's secretary calls for her.

Roxy turns to Irfan, who is entirely immersed in his virtual universe. "Irfan. It's time to go."

He does not stir. She mutters to him on a whim, "I'll be right back. Wait for me here, okay?" Picking up her document folder, she heads to the lawyer's chambers alone.

"Bibi—who are you here with?" Advocate Chandani asks as she enters the office.

"Sir, I am here regarding a probate matter," Roxy asserts.

"Jee bibi. Obviously, you've come to a lawyer for a legal matter. But who and where is your power of attorney?"

"I would like to file directly, Sir. Preferably the fast-track route."

Advocate Chandani does not look amused. "Bibi—the courts don't work according to your desires. If you want to submit an application, come back with a power of attorney. A brother, an uncle, a cousin, a neighbor even—anyone that can show up to the court dates will do. I need to move on to the next client now. You can call my secretary when you are ready."

"But Sir—" Roxy forces herself to stop mid-sentence, positively fuming. The insolence of this mean, mean man! How completely on point with her premonition of doom.

She knows she needs to keep it together and not make a bad thing worse. She walks back out into the waiting room.

Irfan is of course sitting exactly where she left him. She considers making him her power of attorney. Eighteen-year-old Irfan, who has an entire fifty-three days of experience in adulthood, as her advocate in court. An image of Irfan stooping over his phone in the courthouse while the judge continues his proceedings comes to her mind, and she can't help but let out an ironic laugh.

She walks over to him and taps his shoulder, "Irfy—I need your help. Can you please come into Advocate Chandani's office with me?"

Chandani agrees to file the fast-track application. His attitude toward Irfan is only marginally less rude, making Roxy realize he's nothing but the regular brand of douche.

She hopes, for her own sake, that he is at least a competent douche.

"I will submit these to court tomorrow. If the fast-track goes through, we should be able to get the papers to you in two weeks, Inshallah."

Roxy's rage has calmed somewhat by the time she leaves the office, but she realizes she is decidedly not Sahr. Conceding to condescension does not sit right with her at all.

***

It is nearly 8 p.m., but the heat remains relentless. Roxy is dripping sweat as she gets out of the rickshaw in front of her best friend Inara's new apartment complex. Or what she thinks is Inara's apartment complex, in the freaking middle of the boondocks. Her cell phone battery has run out, so she has no way to determine whether she's at the right destination.

She hands the fare to the rickshaw driver and thanks him.

"Bibi—will you be okay here? It will be hard to find transportation at night. If you are only planning to stay for a little while, I can wait to take you back home."

His concern seems genuine, and Roxy decides to share her dilemma. The driver reassures her that he will wait for her until she confirms her coordinates.

Seven minutes later, the door to apartment 15G is opened by a familiar face and Roxy is met with a giant bear hug from her childhood best friend.

"Rooksie! It's been so very long. I can barely believe I am not seeing a ghost!"

Rooksie, the name Inara had christened her with in middle school, has a musical lilt to it. It's the precursor to and inspiration for Roxy, but it's also where Rakhshanda meets Roxy. It is emblematic of her coming of age, of learning to assert herself, and, more importantly, of learning to defy convention. And boy, has that defiance come in handy for her. Rooksie is perhaps the most authentic version of herself.

Meeting Inara is every bit as gratifying as Roxy imagined it being. It feels like not a day has passed since their last meeting, which was at Roxy's father's funeral eight years ago.

They talk late into the night, catching up on the minutest of details from each other's lives. It is just like their teen years when they would talk on the phone until the wee hours of the morning, or until a parent would walk in on them and give them both a deathly scolding.

It is just the same now, but sans the scolding parent.

Inara's face is solemn. "I can't believe it's been eight years since uncle passed away. How has it been for you, to be back after everything that happened then?"

Roxy feels a wave of nausea hit her as she thinks about her dad. She is not sure she can talk about it. But if there is one person who understands the close bond she had with her father, it is Inara.

"I feel betrayed, I guess."

She takes a long pause before continuing, "You remember how hard it was for me to leave for college. This city was my one great love—the zero-zero coordinates of any universe I could envision. No matter where I have lived, I have yearned to return here. But recently, I have felt unanchored and exposed, and worst of all, cheated. Perhaps exactly how you've described—like a ghost of my former self."

Inara puts her arm around Roxy and gives her shoulders a squeeze. "I cannot even imagine. You are brave to have come back, and that too by yourself."

Roxy manages a weak smile for her friend.

"I know I am about to contradict myself. But I think coming back by myself has actually been a very good thing. I've gotten to see the city in a new light. All these years I came back for the people—the friends and family I had left behind. But this time it's different."

Inara raises one eyebrow inquisitively.

"Having lived here since the beginning of time, I never saw this place from the objective perspective of an outsider. And what happened with Abba alienated me from the city. So now, I see things as would a stranger—a stranger holding a strong grudge."

"And that's a good thing, how?" Inara interjects.

"It's a good thing because the score board starts negative. There's no credit for nostalgia or familiarity. Every point has to be deliberately earned through experience."

"Okay…and how has that been working out?" Inara asks, genuinely curious.

Roxy turns to face Inara, who is sitting next to her on the couch.

"I've learned that this magnanimous city of ours embraces everyone with open arms, like the ocean. From my neighbor Sahr to my Uber driver this morning, I've met so many people during this trip who have come here to seek a better life. And this city—it has accepted them, nurtured them, and enabled them to pursue their dreams.

"And the beauty of it all is that this city of outsiders—it's also a city of survivors. It is full of resilient people watching out for each other. Like my rickshaw driver did just now. And I just freaking love that life is a team sport here."

In a lower pitch and with a contemplative expression, she carries on. "I was in no frame of mind to think about anything else when Abba's accident happened. But come to think of it now, there were people, complete strangers, who helped him get to the hospital. And not just that—they visited for several days after, offering to help my mom since she was alone. That sort of compassion and consideration—that is not easy to come by."

Recovering her chirpy, higher pitched voice, she adds, "And how can I forget. I love the wickedly sassy sense of humor people have here. It just makes getting through the day that much more fun! I don't think I realized this before, but that's probably where I acquired my own dry wit from.

"I used to think my feelings towards this place were all driven by nostalgia. That unfortunately leads me down a dark path these days. But the more time I spend here, the more I am discovering a love for this city because of its very spirit, and who it inspires me to be."

***

Three weeks go by in the characteristic way only time knows to operate, sometimes fleeting and other times coming to a screeching halt. Roxy reconnects with old friends and revisits familiar places, imbibing the pleasures of sweet reminiscences.

But she is also hungry to get to know more of this city beyond the ways in which it has intersected with her life. At the community library she meets an illiterate woman seeking help to get her children admitted to a private school so they could have the education she doesn't. At a shop in the mall, she meets a salesperson who had to flee his hometown after an earthquake and chose to make this city his adopted home. In every story she sees the fire that is this city. The fire burning inside each one of them. The fire inside of her. She is this city, and the city is her.

There are still times when she gets mad—angry that this city had to shake the foundation of her being by the senseless cruelty of taking her dear Abba away. But she realizes that places, like people, are also flawed. The wound inflicted on her might never heal, but she hopes it will at least form a solid scab with time.

The resolution of the estate matters continues to be an issue. Chandani turns out to be an incompetent douche who does not submit all the necessary documents, and the fast-track application is denied. So, her father's non-cash assets are inaccessible until the courts can award the certificate of probate to Irfan, who remains their power of attorney in this matter.

Ironically, her mother is far from upset about the state of things. In fact, she gives Roxy the ultimate vote of confidence by saying, "I am so happy to see you're finally mature enough to know how to handle things right. Irfan will make sure we get the paperwork when it is done."

Roxy cannot ignore the implication of her mother's words, but she decides to let it go. She's been able to get her father's pension and cash accounts transferred to her mother, securing her financial future for a good long time to come. And for now, she just wants to focus objectively on these achievements and nothing else at all.

The recent progress, however, also feels bittersweet. Each solved problem is one less practical reason to return here. And the thought of not returning starts a lingering ache in her heart that is anything but practical. She feels like she's cutting off her own roots—with surgical precision.

She wonders if being uprooted enables one to fly higher. She hopes so.

***

Another airport terminal, and a long immigration line. This room is spacious and bright, and nothing like the one Roxy was in three weeks ago. There is one similarity though. Here, too, there are two lines: one for citizens and permanent residents, and the other for visitors.

Roxy looks at the single file queue snaking through three-quarters of the lobby leading up to the sign, *For Visitors*. She turns her passport to the page with her work permit and joins the visitors queue, making the mental calculation that it will take more than an hour to get through.

Her phone beeps incessantly—her friends will keep her company while she awaits her turn.

In just about fifty minutes she reaches the top of the line. The immigration officer has a kind face and deep blue eyes. He looks through her customs declaration form and tells her she forgot to complete Question 15.

"What is the total value of the articles that will remain behind when you leave the country?"

Roxy ponders how much of life is captured through tangible assets. And of that proportion, how might she ascribe value to what she would leave behind in the country she's inhabited for the last dozen years—the approximate dollar value of this identity and lifetime of experiences and relationships.

She responds, as she has every time, "Zero dollars."

"Okay Ms. Rack-shan-duh Ohh-med. Please look straight into the camera and make sure you do not smile."

Roxy nods before setting her head into a neutral position.

The officer stamps her passport with the usual *Admitted for 365 days* remark.

He turns to her and says, "Welcome home."

About the Authors

Amber Bliss (Editor) holds an MFA in Writing Popular Fiction from Seton Hill University and an MLIS from the University of Rhode Island. With a combination of creativity, determination, and a little sorcery, she's managed to combine her passion for writing and tabletop RPGs into her work as a librarian. Amber's days are consumed by stories, whether she's writing them, reading them, or telling them around a table cluttered with dice and character sheets because stories don't only make us werewolves and wizards, they make us human. Her own work can be found in *The Monstrous Feminine* by Scary Dairy Press. You can visit Amber at www.amberbliss.com or follow her @am_bliss on Twitter.

K. Parr (Editor) is the author of a young adult novel and various published short stories in multiple genres, including romance, fantasy, paranormal, science fiction, and humor— all of which star LGBTQIA+ characters. She received her MFA in Writing Popular Fiction from Seton Hill University and her MLIS from the University of Rhode Island in 2017. She currently works as a teen librarian in Rhode Island, and in her spare time, she enjoys reading and writing fanfiction, watching Asian dramas, listening to KPOP, and playing games of all kinds. You can find her online at @kparrbooks on Twitter, @authorkparr on Facebook and Instagram, or her website www.kparrbooks.com.

Maryam Ghatee is an Iranian-American writer. She has built buildings in New York City, Maryland, and Rhode

Island and taught university students. Her passion for writing resurfaced during the pandemic and her work can be found on *The Rumpus*, *Nowruz Journal*, *Santa Clara Review*, and *Wanderlust*. She currently co-leads the Iranian American Cultural Society of Rhode Island and is on the What Cheer Writers Club's B/I/POC advisory committee. She lives in Providence with her husband and daughter. Find her on Twitter @MaryamGhatee.

Gizem Zencirci is an author and political scientist who lives in Rhode Island. Originally from Turkey, she explores questions of community, difference, and identity in her academic and literary work. In addition to writing short stories, she also enjoys painting, textile art, and traveling with her two sons. You can find her at @maviphd on Twitter.

Jowan Nabha was born and raised in Detroit, Michigan to immigrant Palestinian parents. As a teacher and recent graduate from the University of Michigan-Dearborn, she loves telling stories that both her students and her daughters can read and relate to. Jowan considers herself a children's/young adult writer but has recently explored contemporary adult fiction. Her hobbies include traveling, hiking, playing basketball, dancing, and spending time doing those things with family and friends.

Koloud Fawzi Omar Abdul Aziz Tarapolsi, or Kay to her friends, is a Libyan artist, storyteller, and writer. She founded www.ACraftyArab.com to teach children about the Muslim culture and Arab world through educational products and an informational blog. Her unique arabesque quilling artwork has appeared in various galleries and museums, and she has taught it to thousands of students at every age. When she is not writing, she enjoys working on her off-grid tiny house and mountain biking. She lives in Seattle, Washington with her husband, three daughters, and cats Zibda & Dijaja.

Malack Jallad is a writer and student born and raised in Dearborn, Michigan. The eldest daughter of Palestinian immigrants, she often explores her Arab and Muslim identity through her writing and studies. She is a current undergraduate student at Wayne State University, double majoring in Neuroscience and Public Health on the Pre-Med track. After graduation, she hopes to pursue Medicine with a particular focus on minority health. Malack has always had a passion for writing. She is the founder and President of the Creative Writing Club at WSU and was a member of CityWide Poets in high school, where she often performed spoken word poetry. She has published her work in various anthologies and in the school's student newspaper throughout high school and college. To her, writing is an art, an outlet, and a voice. Malack enjoys journaling, nature walks, trying new food places, and spending time with family and friends.

Nayiri Baboudjian Bouchakjian is a writer, educator, and storyteller. She grew up in Lebanon witnessing the civil war, countless assassinations, and the most recent hyper-inflation and economic meltdowns. An educator at heart, she has been teaching English Language and Literature for the past twenty years in different universities in Lebanon. She loves working with teenagers, empowering them and coaching them to become better versions of themselves. Tired of writing just for herself, she started sharing her writing with others after the Beirut port blasts. Since then, her stories and essays have appeared in *Sabeel, Hyebred Magazine,* and *Rusted Radishes*. Her essay "The Ships are Coming" won third prize in an essay competition co-organized by the Oxford Network for Armenian Genocide Research and the International Armenian Literary Alliance. She is currently working on her memoir, which includes stories about growing up in a multiply-traumatized land, being a caregiver to both her parents, and taboo issues associated with body image and mental health.

Alizeh Farhad is a physician, engineer, and educator. She has lived on three continents and is interested in exploring questions of identity and human experience across shifting landscapes through her writing. She has lived in Rhode Island for over a decade, where she is still trying to perfect the art of seasonal living through learning a new outdoor activity from sailing to skiing each year.

CPSIA information can be obtained
at www.ICGtesting.com
Printed in the USA
BVHW090038300922
648202BV00007B/19